When I Was Boudicca

Joann Smith

ISBN: 1499529783
ISBN 13: 9781499529784
Library of Congress Control Number: 2014908868
CreateSpace Independent Publishing Platform
North Charleston, South Carolina

Part One

ONE

---

48 A.D.

Iceni Territory - Southeast Britain

"Tallas." Be alive, Tallas. Please be alive.

His cheek against the ground.

No, I mustn't think that.

A short sword through his chest. His hands pressing the wound. And blood.

No. Why does my mind taunt me with such images?

His face in a grimace, streaked with dirt, and . . .

Are you crying, Tallas? Wait. I will be there. I will be there. Can you hear me coming? Can you feel me coming? Feel me.

"Tallas." Hear me. "Tallas."

I'm coming. Apollo-Belinus, please let him be alive. Keep him alive. Icena, protect him. Esus. Please. I will make offerings. I have not worshipped you well lately, I know; I have not offered enough. But I will. I will give you everything. Please. Please, protect him. Let him be alive.

I will marry you, Tallas. If you are alive, we will not wait any longer. We will not wait for Beltane, and if a winter marriage is to be a barren one as I have been taught, then let it be. What could childbirth bring anyway–my death, as it brought my mother's, and a child whom I would never see, just as my mother never saw me? No, we will not wait for spring. On the next full moon, we will marry.

1

"Tallas." Where are you? Why didn't you tell me of your plan? Your foolish plan. Because I would have stopped you? Yes, I would have. And you might have hated me for it. But you would certainly be alive. Please be alive.

There is that flash of blue again. What is it? No, not a bird. I see now, not a bird. A man. I see him clearly. Running. Escaping? One of your men, Tallas, woaded in blue? Running. Then is it over?

Fool. You are a reckless fool. To challenge Rome? To battle Rome? Did you think you could battle Rome? They will crush you, Tallas. Ask for mercy. They can be merciful. Beg for mercy. Plead.

"Tallas."

TWO

"Captured."

A good word. Not "dead." "Captured." A better word than "dead."

Now finally I will see him. Tallas. Though it has only been two days since I was last with him–and I wish we could go back to that day, the day before yesterday, a day before the rebellion, a day before his capture–it has been forever. Forever spent in waiting. Waiting while Rome took him to the fort. Waiting while my father raged over news of the revolt. "I am king," he'd roared when he heard it was Tallas who had so secretly organized it. "And your dupe. Under my nose, your Tallas plans a rebellion and defies my sovereignty, all the while with my daughter at his side. What kind of a king is that? What kind of a daughter?"

I did not tell him that I did not know. I did not say, "Father, I did not know. Father, I did not betray you." Instead, I was silent. I let him believe that Tallas trusted me enough to tell me. I couldn't bear at that moment to confess to him the truth, that I was excluded from Tallas's confidence, that he did not trust me. You did not trust me, Tallas. I let my father believe I knew. I let him believe you trusted me. But you didn't trust me.

Now there is more waiting. Waiting in this crowd because Ostorius Scapula, Roman governor of Britain, has demanded that we be gathered, that all the Iceni of the village be gathered outside the Roman fort. That my father–Melcut, our king–and his daughter–me– attend.

3

That we be given a place close to the platform that has been built for this occasion.

But I can wait no longer. It is as though my blood will burst my veins. I will run to the fort, push my way through and find him. But on one side of me, my father stands, erect and dignified, a proud king whose set face is meant to calm his people. But it does not calm me, and yet I must stand here, pretending dignity, pretending calm. The king's daughter. And on the other side of me are Carduc and Katha who came to my father at my birth, my mother's death, who have been parents to me, friends to my father. It is Katha's eyes I seek, Katha's eyes which worry as mine do.

Katha.

She offers a glance, reaches across Carduc to squeeze my hand.

Now, there is movement. More guards from the fort. Ostorius Scapula. His man, Lucius. Soldiers. And at last, Tallas.

"Tallas." My first glimpse of him blurs with my tears. The guards yank at his neck chains as if he is a stubborn ox. But he is just a calf, so thin in his nakedness. But a proud calf. Yes, Tallas, I see you struggle to hold your head up. "Tallas."

Captured. But alive. Alive.

Look to me. I am here. I am here. Do you see me? Tallas, I love you.

He is brought onto the platform, he and his brother, Magon, his father, Balin. All chained. All naked. A trumpet is blown, and we obey with silence.

Scapula ascends the platform. "These men," he indicates Tallas, Magon, Balin, "the leaders of your failed rebellion, are responsible for the punishments that will follow– punishments that all of you will bear whether you participated in their rebellion or not."

The word leaps through the crowd. "Punishments." An unbroken murmur of "punishments."

"Rome was brought here to protect you because you could not protect yourselves," Scapula continues. "The cost of that punishment has just gone up. The tributes will be raised."

Wails erupt in waves as the news is passed to those out of range of his voice. "How will we pay?" one asks another hopelessly. "How?"

"And your people will be disarmed."

So, we are to be at their mercy. Be merciful.

Now he shouts over the gasps. "Over the next days, Roman troops will come to your homes, and you will present your weapons. Those Iceni still living in the hills will be moved to the village. All are to reside here now where you can be watched, and all will participate in the building of huts for the hill people." He pauses, and in that moment, I hear the whispered lamentations, "No weapons," and the anxious pleadings for a "merciful Rome."

"These men," again Scapula waves behind him, "have brought this hardship on you. These are the men who have burdened you with the anger and retribution of Rome."

Now Scapula beckons, and Tallas, Magon and Balin are led forward.

A shriek goes up from somewhere in the crowd. A war cry? Yes. Will they attack Scapula, defend Tallas? Yes. My sword—my hand is at the hilt. I am ready. Tallas, I am ready. I will come for you.

A stone hurtles past. Aimed for Scapula, surely. Striking Tallas on the shoulder. A bad throw. But another stone, and Tallas is hit again. Now Magon and Balin. Scapula and his guards step aside. And then it is a storm of small rocks and angry shouts, and Tallas is pelted.

These are my people, his people, turning on him. "Stop it. Stop it."

My father grasps at my arm. Pulls me back. Was I moving forward? And on the other side, Carduc holds me.

But I will go to Tallas. "Let me go." But they hold tighter. "Tallas."

A trumpet blares. Another.

"Tallas."

The guards raise their shields and climb back onto the platform. The stoning ceases. Scapula returns, sneering.

"Do not fear," he shouts. "Rome will finish your work."

My stomach turns. The odors around me are suddenly sickening. My own people, unclean, heavy-breathed. I despise them all, despise the stench of them. "Father." He won't let go of my wrist. "Father." I sink, my arms still held, and vomit.

"But they are not alone in their blame." Scapula keeps talking. "Your king also bears blame."

I rise. Will they stone us, too? "Father." His hand releases my wrist and moves to the hilt of his sword.

"A new king will be named. But first we will teach the rebels what happens when they conspire against Rome."

The guards take them from the platform, yanking on their neck chains, and lead them to the grove. Tallas is pushed against a tree.

"These barbarians..."

Barbarians? Tallas is no barbarian.

"...have raised their swords against Rome who came on the request of your king to serve as protector. The hand that raised a sword against us will not do so again."

"Tallas." My voice, stifled by my fear, is only a whisper. His wrists are unchained, his sword arm raised and pressed against the bark. What is that? "Father?" What objects are those that Lucius is holding? Tallas, I cannot see you, only Lucius's back, Lucius's wide back, then short, sharp motions with his hand.

Lucius steps aside.

"Tallas." He is nailed down by the sword hand to the tree. Now his eyes seek me. "Here. Tallas, I am here." Lucius again. His back blocking me. "Tallas. I am with you. Tallas." What is that glint? Another spike for his other hand? Lucius grabs him by the hair. A swipe.

"Tallas."

Now Lucius stands aside.

"Tallas." His chin against his chest. Quick blood.

"Tallas." His neck slit. Neck that I kissed. Neck where I sought his scent. "Tallas."

I feel myself falling. There is shouting. I am falling. Tallas. Tallas. I am grabbed. Held.

"Stand," my father commands. "If he is yours, stand for him."

Tallas. He is mine. I watch his blood hug his body, watch his blood run into the earth. He is mine.

"Tallas."

THREE

He is dead.

Why do I wake again? Why won't sleep hold me? Hold me and take me to him. When I wake, he dies once more. My first thought, the only thing my body knows: Tallas is dead.

When they pry the nail from his hand, it is as if he is alive when he crumples; there is still motion in him. Bending his knees, he sinks as though weary, against the great trunk of the oak. His head bounces—the nod of a man who cannot fight sleep. Wake up. No, he falls clumsily sideways, his cheek hitting the ground. Then all movement ceases except for the reaching of the dark pool that is his blood.

But I am not there when they pry the nail from his palm. I did not see him fall. I left him. Tallas, I turned and left you. Forgive me. Did you see me? Did you know that I was with you when he killed you? I was there. And then I left. Left you nailed to a tree. Tallas.

Why did you do it, Tallas? And why didn't you tell me? I could have stopped you. And you would still be alive. But you knew that, didn't you? You knew I would try to stop you. You knew I would tell my father-
-to protect him, and you, and all of us. Then there would have been no killings, no punishments. You would still be here. But my interference would have been betrayal to you. "You side with your father," you often said to me. "You side with Rome."

I remember our arguments. We argued so frequently. To me it was just perfume, a bolt of new cloth, a way of keeping my hair from flying

7

in all directions. To you it was a plot to destroy our ways, Rome's method of making us forget what it was to be Iceni. "When you dress like one of them, smell like one of them, you become one of them," you told me.

"I am not one of them," I defended myself. And coiling my hair and wearing their silks didn't make me one of them.

"Weak." You told me I was weak not to resist. You told me my father was weak. I slapped you, do you remember? Yet, you continued your argument. "We could have fought the Belgae," you told me, "when they came from the east, pushing against our borders. We did not need to call Rome in to repel them." But we could not have fought them, Tallas. You want us to be a fighting people, but how long has it been since we have engaged anyone in battle? And the Belgae outnumber us. By now our land would be theirs, and we would be their slaves. "You speak as your father would," you told me. But he was right, wasn't he? We could not have defeated the Belgae alone. And afterward, Rome let us live our lives as long as we pledged allegiance and paid tribute. My father pledged allegiance, Tallas. You broke his word. You broke the trust. And we were prosperous, Tallas. Our mountain ponies are the most agile in Britain, and they trade at a high price. Our crops, with the new methods that keep the soil rich, are plentiful. And the honey your bees produce bring a fair price. But you would say no, this isn't prosperity. "A portion of the crops goes to Rome, a portion of the honey, too, as tribute. We work for Rome," you would say. "We might as well be slaves."

And we argued. And argued.

But I didn't know you would do this. How could I know? Why couldn't you be content, content, as I was?

Where is sleep? Tallas, where are you?

My tongue searches my lips but there is no taste of you. No last kiss. A last kiss. I put my wrist to my mouth, and kiss, pretend it is your neck. But the saltiness of you is not there. The smell of you is not there. Still, I can pretend it is your neck. Kiss. Your neck.

We are by the stream. Your full weight on me. Then mine on you. And yours on me. Rolling. We will roll into the stream. Tallas. Your laugh. My laugh. "I'll fall." "We'll fall," you say. That's it; let me think of gentle times. Let me think of our love, not our arguments.

Remember the first time you touched my hair? We were playing with sticks. I would have played with swords. "I'm not afraid," I told you. "Swords are dangerous," you scolded. "But I need practice," I argued. You watched me practice. Me against the warm air, cutting it, slashing it, fighting well past the time when my arms wanted me to stop. To show you, to impress you. And then with sticks, we battled. "To the death," I declared. You would not have asked for it to go to the death. But in my stubbornness, my pride, I wanted you to know I had courage. I would have won, your stick-sword knocked from your hand. I was aiming at your chest. You reached out, do you remember? I slapped the hand with my stick. "Your hair," you said and reached again, and this time I let you. "Your hair. It holds the sun–the light." Your fingers examined it. "And the warmth," you said. "It's warm." You loved me, Tallas. I saw it then. You loved me. And I had to stand there, so still, when I wanted to jump. I could have jumped. You loved me. And I had to let you know I loved you. How? With a smile? No, that was not enough. I dropped my stick and leaned toward you, put my finger to your lips. How did I know such a gesture? My finger to your lips. This finger. On your lips. Now to my mouth. But there is no taste of you there.

A flash of blue.

I remember it, and now it disturbs my sweet memories. A flash of blue between trees, and it is gone. Then nothing, just the brown of the woods-
-bark and fallen branches, dried needles, hard ground, craggy ground as I ride, searching for you, Tallas. Be alive. Please be alive. But you are not alive now. My pony's breath, clouding the cold air, and my breath, a smaller cloud. And then the blue again, trailing over the brown, and I know what it is. It is defeat. A tribesman, naked and stained blue with woad, darting through the woods, running to save his life, like any other animal who runs to save its life. Then another. And I know your rebellion has failed. I see your warriors running. And then the carts, the wagons, the families coming over the crest of the hill toward me. "Tallas. Does any-one know where Tallas is?" These families who went to cheer their sons, their husbands, even some daughters. Which daughters fought with you, Tallas? Which women did you tell when you would not tell me? They spill down the hill. A wagon careens and topples. The sounds, muffled at first,

then a din—cries and groans, barking and yelping, stomping and snorting. You are defeated. But alive, still alive. Be alive.

In the wagons, children lean rigidly away from the cleaved bodies of their fathers. A rent shoulder. A severed arm. Blood. And mud. And crying.

And I am there forcing my pony against that tide, calling for you. "Tallas." I am calling for you when Leanan finds me. She cannot find her husband, Coel. Is he one of those who ran, one of those blue streaks that disappeared into the woods? Then she'll never see him again. He'll never face her. His shame would be too great. Was one of those blue flashes Coel?

"Leanan, have you seen Tallas?"

"Captured."

But alive.

But not now.

"Captured." A good word, I thought. A better word than "killed." But it is not a good word.

Lucius's back and a swipe. What is that he is drawing across your neck? A dagger? I know it is a dagger.

———

Where is sleep? Why doesn't sleep take me from the agony of these memories?

"Boudicca."

Katha.

"Little one, wake up. You must get up."

I feign sleep. I do not want comforting, though this is so lonely. Maybe later, Katha. Go away, for now, but come later.

"Little one."

Am I still "little one"? A woman who should be preparing for her wedding, a woman who has watched her love die. Our wedding. He would have taken my hand in his. We would be bound as he looked into my face, and I into his. His eyes would be blue—no, green. Changeable eyes. Sometimes blue, sometimes green. What color were they when

Lucius killed you? What color were your eyes when the soldiers pulled the spike from your hand? Tallas. Tallas.

Yes, Katha, I am your "little one." Yes. Take care of me, Katha. "Katha."

"Here. Here. So you open your eyes. I know you were only pretending. Do you think I don't know that you could hear me? Why didn't you answer me? Come, you must get up."

I will not.

"Come. Scapula and Lucius have demanded a meal from your father, and demanded that you be present at the meal." She is gently, but insistently pulling me up.

"No," I protest.

"'No' is not a choice. You are to be at the table. Your father has told me to see to it that you are ready, and you will be ready. Would you defy your father and force him to defy Scapula? Would you do that and leave your father to bear Scapula's anger? Come." She pulls the blanket from me. "You will obey."

"Katha," I plead. Does she need reminding? "They killed Tallas."

"And now they want you at your father's table, and you will obey," she answers in her tone of utter efficiency–but that tone does not conceal her worry.

It is the worry that I respond to. No, I would not bring Scapula's anger on my father. No, I would not risk having my father taken from me. A swipe and blood. No. And worse than defiance, that would be betrayal, and he already believes that I have betrayed him by conspiring with Tallas. I would not torment him any further.

Katha is already at me–a damp cloth to my face, a comb to my hair. She pulls my tunic over my head to replace it with a fresh one, and I am a pliant child, leaning into the familiar smells that are her: honey and vinegar, damp wool and perspiration, coltsfoot which she smokes when she rests and when she worries.

"Good. You wouldn't challenge Scapula or your father, would you?" she coos. "No. Good. I suppose we're to consider it an honor that Scapula himself has asked to have his meal here."

"An honor?"

"Well, you know, the whole Roman troop must be fed, and Scapula has ordered the villagers to provide for them. We could have been assigned any of the soldiers." She goes on, "We'll just give him his meal and send him away. Just do as your father asks. Sit at the table, be polite, and he and his men will be gone soon. No more killing. No more punishments." She pauses briefly. "Carduc will help me serve. I think your father wants him there so that later they can discuss what Scapula said. You know how your father relies on Carduc's counsel."

"What will Scapula say?"

"Nothing, I hope. Nothing more than what he said this afternoon. And maybe he'll rescind some of it. Maybe he'll see that your father had no part in the rebellion and will let him retain the kingship. I don't know. But what's important now is for us to feed him and keep him happy."

Yes, it would be fair to allow my father to hold the kingship. He should not be punished for Tallas's recklessness. But is Scapula fair? I had thought him fair before this. So tonight I will defend my father, and Scapula will listen. I will attest that he knew nothing of the revolt. And later, when Scapula has left, I will tell my father that I, too, knew nothing of the revolt. I will tell him that I am still his Boudicca, that I did not betray him, did not choose Tallas over him. He can love me again, be proud of me.

I decide this. I decide it over and over again while I wait for Scapula's arrival. Scapula and Lucius and their guards. I will do and say what is necessary to get them out of our home before more punishment befalls us. I decide that.

Then they come. And I must look at their tonsured faces and their cropped hair, smell the leather of their uniforms, and the perfumes they use to disguise their natural odors that they, themselves, abhor. I must hear their thin voices–the killers of Tallas. Murderers. A swipe, and blood. A swipe, and blood.

Carduc leans in to offer me wine.

I cover the top of the goblet with my hand. The gesture is enacted before I am even aware that I am considering it. It is instinct, a defense, but now I awake to it, and I let that gesture lead me. "I would prefer mead," I state quietly. My father regards me with stern surprise, and I look away so that I might remain steadfast. I imagine Tallas watching me. You have accused me, Tallas, of adopting Roman ways. Look now, for you I refuse their wine. For you I decide to challenge Scapula.

Katha serves the goose. "No, thank you," I refuse. She nudges me with her elbow. "No, thank you," I repeat, and I do not meet her eyes, either.

My father watches. "Eat, daughter."

But I will not. This is my decision now, to be as Tallas's wife, to choose him. Do you see me choose you, Tallas?

"You must eat for strength," my father urges. But he is clearly not as worried about my gaining strength as he is about my offending our guests.

I am not this brave, to be so defiant, not this staunch that I can hurt my father without disappointing myself. But I think of Tallas in the room, think of him as my husband. My husband in the room. And I am loyal to him. "The Iceni do not eat goose. It is not our way."

My father makes a sound in his throat, a false laugh that comes at me as a warning. "I am afraid, daughter, that you ate goose only last week. The Romans have taught us how tasty a well- seasoned goose can be. We learn from them."

I persist, not without a tremor in my voice and throughout my being. I do not want to choose Tallas over my father, one over the other. But Tallas makes me choose. How can I love him and still do what Rome wants me to do, what my father wants me to do? How can I claim to love him and sit agreeably before his killers? No, love is not that complacent. "Before Rome came," I answer quietly, "we raised geese only for our entertainment and that of the gods, to see them on the lake and in the air. We have sufficient food. We do not need these birds to feed us."

"Boudicca." My father's anger silences me.

Now Scapula laughs. "I shouldn't be surprised that a king who cannot control his people cannot control his daughter, either." Then he grows grave. "You have failed in your duties, Melcut." My father looks steadily at the governor. Scapula pauses and gulps his wine. "Rome has made many friends among the Britons. I thought the Iceni were among those friends."

"I have failed," my father agrees. "But the Iceni who joined the revolt are few in number compared to those who did not. Our tribe still honors the friendship."

"Yes," Scapula says. "Most of your people were wise enough not to participate. Still, you know that such an action cannot go unanswered."

My father says nothing.

"And your daughter," Scapula continues. Now I glance at him. "I understand that the rebel leader was well-known to her."

Tallas.

"Yes," Scapula grins, "I see in her face that it is true."

His eyes are on me, now, Lucius's, too. Lucius's lascivious eyes. Murderous, dark eyes, under thick brows.

"Not a wise choice on your part, Melcut," Scapula accuses.

"My daughter chooses her mate for herself. It is the Iceni way."

"Iceni ways." Lucius laughs. "The ways of barbarians." He holds his cup up for another filling of wine. Carduc obliges.

"What did she know of the rebellion?" Scapula asks.

Without hesitation, my father defends me. "She knew nothing."

Father. He lies to protect me and does not know that he tells the truth.

"I will not tolerate another rebel, even if she is a woman," Scapula warns. Now he eats gluttonously–his small mouth working–as does Lucius, finishing the portions they were given and more. My father and I sit silently, I with only a cup of mead in front of me, my father with a plateful of goose he cannot eat. It is a long night before the Romans are sated.

When at last they are gone, my father dismisses me with his silence, and I am released to my bed.

———

Tallas, did you see me try to be your wife? Did you see me answer Scapula? Did you see me bear my father's anger, his disappointment?

14

Father.

He used to come to me to tell me stories and to rub my aching legs. "You run too hard," he would say. But he was proud of my speed, I remember. "And who did you race today?"

"Tallas, and I won. I am the fastest of the boys and the girls."

"My swift little Boudicca," he would say and rub my legs hot.

"Father. Tell me of my mother who died at my birth."

"You look like her. Your hair is the same color–the color of the sun arriving in the sky. She had a special calm–even in the midst of great activity, there was a quietness around her. She could always soothe me."

"Do I have calm?"

He would laugh. "You, you run too fast for calm to settle on you." He would sit at my bed. I was small and smaller as he talked, as his voice wrapped me inside it like a blanket would, as I drifted to its safety.

Father.

"I combed her hair," he told me.

"You can comb mine," I offered.

"But Katha does such a good combing for you. We'll let Katha do it."

"She is not my mother."

"She is not your mother."

"But like a mother."

"Yes, like a mother."

——

I remember, but now who is this in my room, disturbing my memories? Katha, with a drink? Let me sleep.

"Boudicca."

"Father."

"Sit up."

He used to come to me at night and tell me stories about my mother, and rub my legs. But when my bleeding started, he stopped coming, as is the way with fathers and daughters. Now, tonight, he comes when he has not come in years, and it alarms me.

"Father?"

He holds a sword wrapped loosely in a cloth.

"When I first held you after your birth, it was in this cloth...It was a brighter red, then." The love that was always the sound of his voice is still there. After what I have done, he still loves me.

"Your cheeks took on its brilliance, and I knew you would be strong and full of life." He pauses. "And sometimes reckless."

I will tell him I did not know. I did not betray him. "Father..."

"Stand."

He holds the sword out to me, cradling it as he once did me in those strong arms.

"Take it and raise it," he instructs.

I place the cloth on my bed and slide the sword from its scabbard. It is not long before my arms quake with its heft.

"Once you could hold a sword all day," he reminds me.

Yes, once I could. But on the day Tallas first touched my hair I began to give up the sword. "What is it to be a woman?" I asked Katha that night. She laughed. "To stop fighting with the boys," she answered. But that was not enough. I watched her at the hearth and learned the varied fragrances as she roasted and seasoned pork, and prepared cakes with honey and oats. I learned how to move my fingers on the loom, and all the while, I was losing my strength. "That sword was lighter and shorter." I glance to the wall where my child's sword hangs. But his reproach stings.

"You've grown weak."

Yes. I let the sword droop, tip to the ground. Tallas thought I was weak, too–too weak to be loyal to him, too weak to watch him go into battle. But I am not too weak to be loyal now. I knew nothing, Father. But you will not know that I knew nothing.

"The sword is yours now."

"Mine?"

"When the Romans come to take our weapons, they will not find this one. Dig with me." He squats, rolls away the woven mat next to my bed, and begins stabbing the ground there with his dagger, the dagger that is always strapped to his side.

"But this is your sword. Carduc forged it for you when you were named king." I remember Carduc making swords. I will think about it later, in bed again, when there is nothing to do but think. But now I do not want this sword. I know what the passing of the sword means. But he is not near enough to death to pass it. And I do not want to be queen.

"I am no longer king. It is appropriate that the sword be passed down to the first-born. That is our way, too," he says, reminding me that he is not in need of the lessons in our ways that I offered at dinner. "Keep it safe. The time will come when you will need it."

"Father, won't you need it? If a time comes..."

"When the time comes, it will be your time."

"But the passing of the king's sword means that I am to be queen. Rome will not name me queen."

"No."

"Then, father..."

"A time will come when you will need a sword. Until then it will lie in the ground. Dig with me."

Silently, me, with my fingers. He, with his dagger. Until a deep cut opens before us.

"Place it in the ground."

I wrap it in the cloth of my birth and lay it in the opening. We cover it with dirt, smooth the place with our hands, pull the mat back over the spot.

"Good. Now sleep again."

Nothing else, Father? Won't you stay with me a while? Tell me a story of my mother?

"Good night."

"Good night, Father."

But when he leaves, I am not alone. The sword is there, drawing my thoughts to it. I saw it made. Carduc showed me.

He melts the iron into a liquid, then pours it into a mold the shape of a sword's blade. And he heats it again, and teaches me the hot metal's various shades of blue. "This will make a stronger blade; this, a more flexible one." He lets me help him collect the mares' urine–a

17

wash in the urine cools the blade and tempers it. Then he grinds the edges sharp–both sides, so the sword will cut two ways. And he engraves the blade, but I am bored–the movements of his chisel are too slow for me–I must run. Later, he shows me. An intricate pattern dances across the blade's surface. "How did you do it?" But when he works the other side, I'm impatient again, and later, again, the design appears as though by some magic.

My father's sword, buried.

My father's sword, buried in my room.

FOUR

"Boudicca."

Again, I wake. Again, Tallas is dead.

I turn away from Katha who calls to me again. Why won't she let me have what I want– endless sleep, release from this waking.

"I know you hear me," she says impatiently. "You must get up. Scapula and his soldiers are coming for the swords. You can't be in bed when they come," she worries. "They'll want to look in every room for weapons, your room, too. You can't be lying here. It wouldn't be proper. And besides that," she lowers her voice, "I saw the way Lucius looked at you."

I saw the way he looked, too. I know what Katha is fearing. Lucius, forcing himself on me. My mind makes quick, revolting pictures, and recalls the stories I heard as a child, stories told by older girls who used hushed voices, stories of fierce battles ending with the victors satisfying themselves on the women of the defeated tribe.

I turn back to Katha and get up, cursing Scapula for denying me my bed, forcing me to participate in this life that I no longer want.

As she fusses at me, Katha whispers the news she's heard. "Scapula has allowed Tallas's body to be buried. He was threatening to have him dragged into the woods and abandoned."

"Katha..."

"Shh, no, don't worry. He is buried. His spirit is released to the otherworld. I think Scapula wants the peace back. He didn't have to allow the burial, you know. But I believe he wanted to remind us of his generosity."

But now I see Tallas lying in the woods, unburied, the way Scapula threatened. Lying alone, denied a death ceremony, and his spirit trapped as a result, trapped here endlessly, restless and wandering, a thing of dread, not of this world or the other. But Scapula, it seems, was not so brave as to dare Tallas's spirit to wander.

"But was he buried with a sword?" I worry.

She shakes her head. "I've heard that he was not."

So, this is Scapula's generosity; he sends Tallas to his grave unarmed and without honor for the next world.

"My dagger," I demand, sickened. Katha hesitates, shows her disfavor in the way she pulls her lips into a tight line, but regards me for another moment and decides not to try to dissuade me. She retrieves the dagger from the chest, and I strap it at my waist.

Shortly, the Romans arrive. My father presents his swords but Lucius is unsatisfied.

Look at him, I command myself, straight at him or he will suspect the deception, the buried sword. Straight at him, filthy creature who killed Tallas. Tallas. Lucius's back. A swipe. And blood.

From the hearth wall he removes a socketed axe and a spear, then, appetite whetted, he leads the soldiers toward my room.

Father. I steal a quick glance at him. But his eyes, more disciplined, do not meet mine. He watches the men move toward my room, watches with a face of calm annoyance, not a face that could give away his guilt, not a face that frets over discovery.

But I fret. Is Lucius kicking the mat aside? Does he see where the earth was dug and smoothed? Imprisonment for us? Death?

He returns with a sword. But–a whimper of relief escapes me–it is my light sword.

My father snorts. "It's a child's sword." Lucius moves toward him, points the blade at his throat.

Father.

"But it draws blood, does it not?"

"Take it," Scapula instructs.

My sword. Now my hands want to hold it once more.

"Where is the metal worker?"

My father leads them into the yard, indicates Carduc's work hut. I follow with Katha.

Carduc steps out of the hut; the Romans enter. His molds and tools are kicked and thrown, but Lucius and his soldiers emerge without a weapon. Strange. I have seen weapons there, many weapons. Next they prowl the hut where Carduc and Katha sleep, and from there they remove two swords, Carduc's dagger and Katha's, and a sling.

"The sling and the dagger are needed for hunting," Carduc protests.

Katha gasps as he is shoved to the ground.

Scapula directs his soldiers to the huts of our field workers and herd tenders. Greedy Lucius leads the way.

We wait and wait. And wait, until at last they ride past us with a cart of weapons between them. Carduc and Katha return to his work hut to put his tools back in place. My father takes my hand and leads me back to the house, to my room where our eyes anxiously go to the mat that is undisturbed. Yet, I am not satisfied—I want to throw the mat aside, dig into the ground to be sure the sword is still there, but I don't dare. Their presence is still palpable. They are here though not here.

My father, seeing me turn my head to a sound, seeing the fear on my face, takes the lighting torch and holds it to the fire until it catches, then moves it in front of him, casting its light in this corner, that corner.

Does he feel it, too? Does he feel watched? Even without their eyes on us we are watched. And to be watched is to be afraid. My father is afraid.

But of what? What is there to fear now? All that can happen has happened. There will be nothing more. Nothing more can hurt us; nothing more can hurt me. I can look forward to long days in my bed. Long days with memories of Tallas.

But Katha returns, and won't let me be. Now that I am up, she wants me to stay up, away from my bed. "You weren't thinking of going back to bed, were you? Not in the middle of the morning. Too much sleep will make your blood lazy. Come, sit with me by the hearth." I comply, and her busyness does comfort me.

But sleep insists, and soon comes over me again. It wants me, and I want it. Long sleep. Still, Katha won't let me yield. She walks me into the yard, into the cool air, so that I might be revived.

We watch Carduc leave his work hut and walk quickly toward the village.

"I hope he is careful," Katha frets.

Careful at what? But right now, I do not want to speak to ask it. I do not want Katha to answer and to force me into conversation, and let conversation force my sleepiness away. Silence and sleep; those are the companions I want now.

And at last Katha allows me to return to these companions.

Welcome companions. My bed and silence, and soon, sleep. Soon sleep. And Tallas. Sleep and dreams and Tallas. My Tallas. Come sleep. Come Tallas.

But my father's sword is companion now, too. And it is not a silent one. *A time will come*, it bodes. *You are not worthy*, it chides.

A wash in mares' urine. Sharp on both edges. Carduc etches the blade.

Tallas, come to me. And sleep.

But the sword crowds the room, keeps sleep out. What does it want from me? What does my father want? The only sword in the house is here in my room. The only sword in the village, here in my room. My father's sword in the ground. Where is Tallas?

Restless night. Sleep comes near, then flies. Comes near again, settles, but lightly, teasingly, then is disturbed and abandons me again. Tallas, comfort me. But what comes is not the gentleness of our love, but the agony of his death. Swipe and blood. His blood. And my anger. Why couldn't you accept things as they were, Tallas? And visions of him in battle as Rome rallies its force, and visions of him in the ground without a sword. Take my father's sword. He and my father's sword in the ground.

———

Then, Katha, again. Smelling of herself. Has this miserable night passed? Has sleep given me all it will for now? Am I to give up my bed before I could even dream? No dreams. No sweet memories to soothe me. Only Tallas in the ground. Tallas bleeding. Where is our love?

"A new king is to be named today," Katha says, already wiping my face with a cloth.

I'm not a child. I snatch the cloth.

"Scapula has ordered that you and your father be present at the announcement."

I will not answer. I want silence, the silence that was denied me last night, I will take now.

"Get up now. Your father is waiting."

I hear her open the chest at the foot of my bed.

"Here," she says, as she unfolds the cloak, "you'll wear this."

I leap from the bed and take it from her–the cloak that was to be my wedding cloak– woven of sheep wool and goat hair, dyed with a woad that I mixed with berries. It holds the light in varying ways, as I hoped it would–blue now, then green, the inconstant color of Tallas's eyes.

"That is for Tallas," I say, abandoning my silence. Tallas. His name aloud. Tallas, like a sweet cake in my mouth. "That is for Tallas," I repeat so I can say the name again. Perhaps I do not want silence, after all. I do want to say and hear that name. Tallas. Let Tallas be my language. "This cloak was for our wedding. I will not wear it for Scapula. Bring me the brown one."

"But, little one, the brown one is so dull. Don't you want to look nice for your father? It's the last time he will be seen in the village as king."

"The brown cloak," I demand.

She clucks her tongue and mumbles about my stubbornness, but then goes on with her nervous chatter. How could I think that with Katha there could be such a thing as silence? "Carduc hears that Prasutagus will be named."

"Prasutagus?" I ask. "My father's friend? The council member?"

"He has learned Rome's ways and has profited from them. Rome trusts him. He will be loyal."

I nod. "And he has no daughter whose lover might betray him." Again, I strap my dagger at my side. Though the Romans may not consider it a weapon worth confiscating, it feels like protection.

————

The ceremony outside the Roman fort is brief. Prasutagus is named; my father is disgraced. The people cheer, as they think they should, but it is without hope. They have absorbed the impact of their punishment and are already exhausted at the prospect of higher tributes, and are cowed by the disarming. A king is named who can carry no sword. And there are still men dying from their battle wounds.

Scapula, it is learned, will leave our territory and return to the west to pursue Caratacus. Run, Caratacus. Caratacus of whom Tallas spoke. A Catuvellauni prince who turned against Rome. Forced to flee when his people would not join him in his struggle to oust Rome from their territory. Why do our people choose Rome before Tallas, before Caratacus? "He travels in the west," Tallas told me, "inciting hatred for Rome, teaching people what Rome's intentions are." I listened. I can hear his voice exhorting me to admire Caratacus. A fool, I thought. And he'll be caught. And killed. Now Scapula has sworn to make himself a reputation on Caratacus. Run, Caratacus. But you will be caught, and your wife will lament as I do.

Lucius will leave, too, and most of the cohort–Scapula would put all his soldiers to hunt Caratacus. All these soldiers on one man. Such is Rome's vanity. But we will not be left unguarded. "We will set up a colony of veterans at Camulodumnum," Scapula announced. In Trinovante territory to the south. "From there, you will be carefully monitored. And the fort here will be enlarged so it can house a contingent of soldiers. You will assist in the expansion of the fort here, and in the building of homes in Camulodumnum for the veterans. And work on the baths and the temple there will proceed." Temple. Built to a man.

"They worship men," Tallas warned me. A man. Claudius. Not yet dead. "They call him a god." Why didn't I see the evil of Rome then? I should have seen it when you told me, Tallas. "You just don't want to see it," you accused me. I see it, Tallas. I see it now. All of their evil.

———

Scapula informs my father that there will be one more meal that we must endure with him. One more meal, and then my bed, again. Scapula gone, and then my bed, and thoughts of Tallas. But will Tallas come? Or are all my future nights to be as last night was? Is the sweetness of our love gone, and only the agony of his deed and his death left for me?

My father welcomes the Romans into the house they so rudely searched just a day ago. Hospitality, that is our way, too.

"Will your daughter drink with us this time?" Scapula asks with a threatening smile.

I will not drink, though it is futile. My defiance only entertains him; I can see that, and when he grows bored of it, I will know.

Katha brings the wine, and after they drink–I let a cup be poured for me, though I do not put it to my lips–Scapula announces the reason for his visit. "It is about your daughter that we have come."

So, already they have tired of me. But why this fear in me? They could kill me, send me to Tallas. That is what I want. Not this life. So why am I afraid?

"Prasutagus is in need of a wife."

A wife? I open my mouth to protest but my father is already speaking for me. "She will not marry Prasutagus."

"I will not."

Scapula laughs. "Your daughter has shown affection for the rebel, Tallas, and it has been the way among the people of this island that a woman might fight as a man does. Therefore, I am concerned, and the same concern arises among your own people, that she will attempt to carry on his rebellion."

"We have no weapons," my father reminds Scapula.

"No," Scapula agrees. "Still, we want assurance of her cooperation."

"She will cooperate," my father promises. Then he turns to me. "Drink the wine."

I do, all my earlier conviction gone. I will drink wine, eat goose, coil my hair if that will protect me from this marriage. I cannot marry anyone but Tallas.

"A nice demonstration," Scapula scoffs. "But your word, Melcut, and her sip of wine are not sufficient guarantee. She will marry Prasutagus." He says it plainly, as a matter of fact.

"I will not."

This time it is Lucius who laughs. Scapula sits calmly, unmoved by my anguish.

"Please."

"Please," Lucius mimics.

"I think Lucius has an interest in you." Scapula's face is hard and mocking. "Would you rather let Lucius have you?"

My father bolts from his chair, and Lucius rises, but with the raising of a single finger, Scapula orders Lucius down. My father calls for his guard–but what protection is an unarmed guard–and for Carduc. "Take her to your hut," he commands Carduc. "Keep her there."

Scapula does not prevent me from leaving.

Katha joins us, and I am hurried from the room and from our home. "I will not marry him. I will not marry him."

Inside their hut, Carduc stokes the hearth fire while Katha wraps me in one of the woven wool blankets piled on the mats that serve as her bed.

"I will not marry Prasutagus," I repeat. "I will not." But the words feel impotent. "I will not."

"You will do what has to be done," Carduc answers in the voice he uses when he acts as a father, when he decides sternness is called for. His tone is not unkind but it gives me no hope, either.

I will not. I will not.

When the fire is high, Carduc squats on the floor next to me. "Hasn't your father honored you with the passing of his sword?" he asks.

I look at him, puzzled. What has his sword got to do with Scapula's demanding my marriage to Prasutagus? "Yes," I answer so that Carduc will continue and explain how one relates to the other. But he says nothing else, and leaves me with wild suppositions. Is this the time my father told me would come? Am I to use the sword to kill Prasutagus? Scapula? Is that how I repay the honor of being passed the sword?

Katha busies herself, emptying a small bucket of milk into the cauldron suspended there. Tallas. Do you see what you've done? How could you leave me to this?

The milk bubbles, and Katha shakes one of her many jars over the pot, then dunks a cup and hands it, dripping, to me. "Sweet milk."

I won't drink.

"Then you'll help me." Earlier in the month, when the ground began to soften, the grain that was stored through the coldest months in the deeply dug pits outside the house was retrieved. Now, it lay in sacks around the room. She digs a bowl into one of the sacks, scoops up some of the grain, puts the bowl in my lap, and hands me a grinding stone so I might crush the grain. Activity. Katha's ready answer to fear and sorrow.

"I will not marry him." My movements with the stone are slow and unproductive, and after some time she takes the bowl and stone, and I hear the small sound of mashing of husks.

I will not marry him.

It is long or not long, I cannot tell, before the guard knocks and instructs Carduc that the Romans have gone, and I am to be brought back.

Katha pushes her strength into the bowl of grain a final few times, and I wish she would continue. I would listen to that sound forever if it would keep me from knowing what has been decided for me.

"I will not marry Prasutagus."

She takes my arm. "Your father wouldn't do anything to hurt you or the tribe. Let's hear what he has to say."

What could he say? I have disappointed him, but enough for him to agree to this arrangement? No. He would not agree. And if he does–but

27

he would not–I will defy the order. I will not marry Prasutagus. They can't force me to marry him.

He is sitting and does not even look up as I enter. Look at me. One fist is on the table, the other is at his mouth. The curve of his back is that of an old man. Scapula must have forced him into some humiliating compromise for the sake of sparing me from this marriage. But I will help him bear it. Whatever burden Scapula has placed on him. I will help him. I will care for him for the rest of his life for saving me from this marriage. And then so clearly, I understand the meaning of the sword. He has passed his strength to me, and now I will be his protector as he was mine. I will care for him. Yes. That is my duty, the duty of the sword, to care for him. "Father." I put my hand on his shoulder and come up alongside him.

Coins. A shiver shoots through me. What are these coins on the table? "Father?"

His voice is hollow. "You will marry Prasutagus."

"Father?"

He does not answer.

I continue to regard the coins. "Have you sold me?" I try to understand their meaning.

"He left coins, I did not sell you."

"But this is what they paid for me?" Now my hands are on the coins. "A moment ago I was worried over what you might have had to do to save me from this, what burden you might have had to bear. But now I see how foolish I was." I send two fistfuls skittering across the wide wood of the table. "Then Tallas was right. You've told me it was mercy. All those Iceni children sent to Rome. You sold them. And now you've sold your own daughter."

He answers hoarsely. "Those children would have been drowned in the river by their own mothers. You know that. You've seen a drowning yourself. Have you forgotten how frightened you were at that sight? But that woman could not provide for that child. In Rome, that child would have been given food and a place to sleep."

I remember the sight–the woman crouched in the water. Blood rising to the surface. Her cry as the child dropped from her into the river, her arm, scooping it up, and then her dagger, severing the cord, and the small, bloody body floating, floating away from its mother.

And now I am severed, too.

He continues, "Those children that I sent to Rome will work in Roman households and will be well-treated. Even educated. And their mothers who could not feed them can now provide for their other children with the money Rome paid."

"Those children sent to Rome will be slaves," I cry.

"No."

"Yes. Yes. Everything you've told me about Rome is a lie. And everything Tallas told me is true. He told me, Father, he told me that you sold children as slaves. I defended you. I said it was mercy. Just as you've told me. But it wasn't mercy. It was just another way to please Rome. And now you've sold me. Your own daughter to please Rome. Tallas was right. And if he were here now, he would prevent this. He would kill Scapula. He would kill Prasutagus, too. He would kill you if he had to, but he would never see me sold."

A dark wing flaps across my cheek. I throw my hands up to protect my eyes. A crow? A creature sent from the gods as a punishment for my boldness?

"You will not speak to the king that way," Carduc chastises me, and I realize it was his quick dark hand, blackened and coarse from working with metal and flame that crossed my face.

"I am Tallas's!" I shout. "I will be no other's." Say something, Father. Say something that will change this. Say that you will kill Scapula. Why do you say nothing? "I will not marry Prasutagus!" I shout. "Do you hear me?" My eyes travel the room wildly as if there is a solution there if only I could spot it. Katha, alarmed, approaches me. "Don't come near me," I cry, moving around the table. "Don't touch me. Don't touch me again. None of you will touch me." I pound my leg with my fist, and sob.

My father raises himself from his chair; Carduc is nearing, too. In a moment I will be corralled, subdued, stopped from having my rage, stopped from striking myself when it feels like resistance, the only resistance I can offer. I will resist.

My dagger. Quickly, it is in my hand. Carduc stops moving.

"Boudicca." It is my father and Katha at once.

A swipe. And blood. I see blood before I feel the throb.

And now I let them come to me. Katha. Carduc. My father. Katha goes and comes back with a cloth. She tears strips and hands them to Carduc; he wraps my arm tightly.

"It is not deep enough to need sewing," he assures my father. Then to Katha he says, "Take her to her bed."

My bed. Tallas. Will you come to me, Tallas? I need you now. Don't abandon me as my father has. Come to me. Come, Tallas.

"Is it so bad that you would hurt yourself?" Katha asks tearfully as she helps me to the bed.

Why does she have to ask? Yes, it is so bad, and I am glad to have felt the sharpness of a dagger against my skin the way Tallas felt it. A swipe. And blood. It brings me nearer to him.

Carduc comes with a cup; Katha puts it to my lips. One of Carduc's mixtures. It will ease me, make me sleep. I drink. Come, sleep. Come, Tallas.

———

Sleep and wake.

Sleep and wake. Tallas, where are you?

———

On the next day, Katha quietly brings me the news. The marriage is to take place in two days.

I could stare past her, let my mouth go slack. I could start to relieve myself in my bed, let my hair knot. I could shriek, and then go silent. Shriek again. She would think me mad and would bring others to witness it. "She screams and then says nothing. See how she stares. At what? It is as if she sees something there." I could talk to that something there. The marriage would be called off.

30

Katha sits at my bed, strokes my arm. "Are you hungry?" she asks. Then she coos, "It won't be so bad. Prasutagus is a good man. And once you are married, Scapula and Lucius will be gone. Lucius has fulfilled his term of service, you know, and could stay behind here if he chose to. You've seen how he looks at you. Without weapons for your father to defend you with, Lucius could have you right here in this house, and your father could not stop him. But Scapula has promised to take him with him as soon as you are married."

My father could stop Lucius. I could stop him. I have a dagger. I could kill him. I can see the dagger at his throat. Swipe. No, not so quickly as a swipe. Slower. Tearing. Fold of flesh by fold of flesh. The dagger dragging.

Katha dabs at her eyes. "Carduc has come to speak to you. I'll go get you something to eat. You have to eat."

Carduc. His blackened hand. I turn away.

He does not sit on the bed the way Katha did. "You are to be queen now and must think of the tribe before yourself. Your father gave you his sword because he believed you had strength. But the sword also demands duty. And you must honor it by accepting your duty. Your duty is to be queen."

And to be queen, I must marry.

Carduc continues, "The people will look to you for your example. You may continue to drink mead and disdain wine, refuse goose; you will dress in the bright colors of the Iceni. As long as you appear as a loyal wife to Prasutagus and do not interfere with the collection of the tribute, Rome will be assured that they have broken you. But you will not be broken. And our ways will not be forgotten. It was brave of you to refuse Katha's goose when Scapula came to dine. Your father said so. Rash and defiant. But brave. He passed the sword to you that night, didn't he? So, go with dignity to your duty."

Silence follows. I don't know if Carduc is still in the room or not. I don't want to turn to look, don't want to meet his eyes and have him believe that I have accepted what he calls my duty. So my father thinks me brave? And I am to go on refusing wine? But what will that do? Remind us how to be Iceni? And what is it to be Iceni? To accept punishment with dignity? To marry whom Rome chooses. To have one's life dictated by Rome, that is what it is to be Iceni. Me, in my colors, drinking mead, refusing goose, married to a man I will abhor. Married.

In two days, I will marry. That is the horrible truth. I can deny it once more. I will not marry Prasutagus. But I did not believe those words even the first time I said them. I hoped with those words and fought with those words, but I did not believe those words. It will come, like the morning will always come. Inexorably. I cannot stop it. I am nothing against Rome. And I am not brave enough to put my dagger in my heart. I will marry. But I will not love. Those words, I can believe. I promise, Tallas. I will not love. And Prasutagus will be sorry. I will be no wife. From this bed to another bed. That's all the marriage will be. I will sleep through it, Tallas. I will call to you in my sleep. In Prasutagus's bed, I will call to you. I promise.

Dignity. It fails me in the night. Tallas, how could you have left me to this? See what your rebellion brought. Yes, I am still capable of wanting you to have done nothing, to have accepted Rome's presence even now when I know what Rome is. Even now when they have taken you away from me, I could still wish that you had done nothing. I still wish I could have stopped you. How could you be gone? How could you have left me to this? Where are you? And the sword that has doomed me to my duty is no comfort. What else will it demand of me as it lies in the ground? What other duties will it call me to?

But my cloak. Yes, that will give me comfort. That will bring me Tallas. Yes. Here it is. The color of his eyes even in this darkness. Come. Cover me in my bed. His warmth. His eyes. Blue or green?

———

Dignity. On the morning of the cursed wedding, I rise while it is still dark. I will do this, as Carduc has advised, with dignity. Tallas. This should have been our wedding day. Then let me wear my cloak. Let me pretend I am going to you. You are with me.

When Katha comes, she is disappointed that I have readied myself without her help, but seeing my cloak out pleases her. "So vibrant," she says, touching it. Now I let her comb my hair. "It covers your back," she observes. "Shall I coil it?"

"No. Leave it loose."

Around my neck, I place the torque that was my mother's. These cool gold braids knew her; they knew the rise and fall of the voice that soothed my father; the dignity of a queen. They know, too, the horror of Tallas's death. I wore it to his killing. Another vow. I will wear the torque every day. From it, I will learn my mother's calmness, and her natural dignity, and every day it will remind me of what Rome did to Tallas. I will never forget.

Before we leave the room my eyes wander over the mat. My father's sword would be left there to rust in the ground. How could I recover it while I lived in Prasutagus's house? Then can it make no more demands? But still I will regret having to leave it–my father's sword, his gift, his pride in me. And Katha will be left, too. She must stay here with Carduc who must stay with my father. "Katha." When she wraps her arms around me, we cry. "Katha, I don't want to go." A tight embrace, and then she loosens her arms. No, don't let go. But she releases me, wipes my face. There, and I am to stop crying. Dignity. My duty.

She presents me to my father who is waiting outside at the chariot. Though his face has hollowed over the last few days, he is imposing in his finest cloak–purple and lined lengthwise and across with red fibers, held closed at his shoulder with a great gold clasp. His faded brown hair is combed to his shoulders, and his moustache that extends below his chin has been twisted at the ends and oiled. The pony, too, is finely arrayed. Her bronze plating, dark now, will soon reflect the rising sun, as will the red and blue enamel studding on her reins. Her head covering with its swooping etchings has the effect of elongating her eyes, lengthening them to the center of her head so that she looks less a creature of this world than another. I believe my appearance pleases my father; he announces his approval with a slight nod.

He takes my hand and helps me up, and we ride silently toward the village with the first streaks of light breaking open the dark sky. My wound, hidden in the sleeve of my cloak, is already mending, and the skin there pulls. The sting is a welcome reminder of my resistance to this thing I am about to do. I did resist, Tallas.

Carduc and Katha follow, Carduc leading the calf that will be the offering. An offering. That's what I am. An offering to Rome.

Who has chosen this spot? My tree. Carduc? Carduc, yes. Carduc, who brought me here as a child. "This will be your tree. An ash. Come here to worship and to think. The tree will learn your spirit. The gods will hear you." I sat with my back against the trunk, speaking my prayers and my hopes out loud, making my small offerings of cakes and grains. And each year, at Beltane, in celebration of the end of the dead season and the coming of the new leaf life, I brought strips of colorful cloth to throw up so the branches could catch them. I can remember throwing the colors at my tree. Blue. Green. But I was a child then, and it has been a long time since I worshipped with that kind of enthusiasm. It has been a long time since I've sat at my tree. And maybe this is my punishment for loving Tallas so much that I was distracted from my prayers. Forgive me. Apollo-Belinus. Teutates. Esus, Epona, Icena. Forgive me.

My father dismounts and takes my hand, bringing me toward Prasutagus. I will not look. Carduc leads the calf to the tree where Prasutagus, too, has brought an offering–an unconcerned pig. They have summoned a Druid, though Scapula could have pronounced us married. But I see how clever he is, how vicious. A marriage made by Scapula could not bind us. Yes, guards could hold me at Prasutagus's house, but the marriage, in the eyes of the Iceni, would not be binding. But with a Druid attending it will be recognized.

He is shaved except for a band of hair stretching across the crown of his head from ear to ear; his hands and feet which extend from his robe of rough white cloth are marked in intricate patterns of blue woad–the blue of Tallas's fleeing warriors. Uttering strange words, he raises a sharp dagger, killing the calf with a single motion. If I asked him, he would open the calf, spill its entrails onto the ground, and read my future in the pattern they formed. But I will not ask him, and without my asking, my future cannot be told to me. I know my future;

it is hateful to me. If I am to be told stories of my life, I want my past told, where there was love, not my future.

Scapula and Lucius look on the Druid warily, alert and clearly resentful of the power they are in the presence of. After the pig is killed the priest binds my hand to Prasutagus's with a white cord–Tallas, Tallas, I say your name over and over to myself, but it is not you–calls on the gods to protect us and render us fruitful, weds us and takes away all my hope.

I am taken by this husband onto his chariot and brought back to his house for a celebration. I am to celebrate. Though invited, Scapula does not attend. As king, Prasutagus will be judged by his hospitality as all kings are, and he has provided seemingly limitless amounts of food and drink, and it is without restraint that the Iceni guests revel at his round table, eating ravenously of the beef and pork, drinking heartily of the tankards of beer and mead, as well as wine. I watch silently, these people, my people who threw stones at Tallas, celebrate a wedding I do not want. Enjoy themselves. Laugh. So heartily. So heartily. And eat and drink some more. And laugh. So contagiously, but I will not smile. Prasutagus will not see me smile. The Iceni. This is who they are when Rome isn't turning them against one another–a lusty people who relish their own company.

My father sits to the right of Prasutagus, normally a seat of honor, but for Melcut, respected king just days ago, it is a place of disfavor. He eats and drinks only enough not to offend his host and leaves soon, bowing his head to me as he kisses my hand, treating me as a queen rather than a daughter. I follow him away from the table.

"Father." He clasps my hand in his, and I feel the strength of him, diminished, but still solid. Take me with you. Don't leave me. He releases my hand, I let him go. I do not run after him. Father. I watch until he is gone and then watch longer. I do not want to turn, turn and enter what is now my life.

"Boudicca."

But he makes me turn, and now I look fully at him. Though nearer my father's age than mine, he is not an old man. His hair, the color of dry earth, is without gray. He stands straight and sure, taller than Tallas and broader, and I can see how he is a man, and Tallas, just a boy. I prefer the boy. He extends a hand. I will not take it.

"Boudicca." Gently. His hand. "Come."

That night I share his bed. He lets me cover myself with my cloak. I close my eyes and think of Tallas. Tallas and I on the riverbank, rolling and laughing. Tallas. But he is not Tallas. Even with my eyes shut tight, he is not Tallas. Even with my cloak clenched in my hand, he is not Tallas.

In the morning, Carduc brings a message. My father is dead. I am taken to the house where I find him on his bed, still and peaceful as though in sleep. A cup stands on the floor nearby, and when I pick it up and smell the strangely sweet fragrance, Carduc watches my face until I understand.

"Poison," I say.

He nods.

I do not ask if Carduc mixed it for him or if my father mixed it himself.

I am reminded again of the blue-skinned men darting through the forest after the failed revolt. By now their shame has caught up to them. How many found a way with a dagger or poisonous berries or herbs to do what my father did? I ask Carduc nothing more. My father's action will be accepted by the tribe, and respected–he was a king who was forsworn. This death was the only honor left him.

I didn't know, Father. I didn't betray you. I didn't know.

Prasutagus comes to me again that night, gently as the night before, and with sorrow for my loss. In my loneliness, I let him hold me.

FIVE

8 Months Later

I will not scream. This pain will tear me apart, but I will not scream. And I will die as my mother did. I can feel this child taking my life for herself. As I must have done to my mother. Did she feel her life go? Did she fight? No. She let me take it. Quietly, as Katha has told me. And I will give my life quietly now, with dignity. Dignity. That old demand.

"Soon," Katha promises.

Thank the gods she is here with me. Wasn't Prasutagus kind to bring her to me after my father's death? She and Carduc, with me again. Wasn't he kind? He is so kind. I hate his kindness. Another pain. I will die. But I would like to see the child's face, even just once to know what that face held. She is not yours, Prasutagus. For all your kindness and all your gentleness, she is not yours. She was already in me when they killed Tallas. She was with me when they killed her father. A witness. If I die, this baby will not know that her father was Tallas. Not Prasutagus. Not Prasutagus. "Tallas."

Katha shushes me. "The king is waiting outside."

I am not my mother. I cannot be quiet. The pain... this child is ripping me, and I don't want to die. "Tallas."

"Shh."

"No." No *shh*. No dignity. "Tallas." Again, "Tallas."

SIX

Carduc comes when Prasutagus is out. He is out often. "The people need to see their king," he says. My father ruled the same way. Visibly. But they do not need to see their queen, not as often, anyway. Sometimes Prasutagus wants my company, and I go with him. But he never insists. He is kind. I wish he weren't, it would make hating him so much easier. "Is there something you need?" he asks. "Something you want?" If I ask, I can have what I ask for. But I don't ask. I don't want his kindness. Only for Katha and Carduc, and he didn't even make me ask. "I will have Katha and Carduc brought here," he said. "Would that please you?" I only had to nod.

Carduc comes. The baby's eyes have not settled into this world yet. They are still the fluid black of the darkness she has passed through to get here. And yet Carduc comes. So soon after the birth. I don't complain. I let him dig up the sword, moved here by some stealth of his to this room I share with Prasutagus. When? I don't know, but soon after my father's death, and he has had me practicing with it ever since.

"You will do what has to be done," Carduc said of the proposed marriage to Prasutagus. "Dignity," he wanted. Duty. I did not expect him to come to me and urge me to honor my father's sword by practicing with it, dishonor my husband by furtively practicing with the sword. But I have been glad for the activity and for the honor I can pay my father's memory, and glad, too, because it is a way of resisting, a way of defying Prasutagus even though he doesn't know I defy him.

And now Carduc comes. "It has been weeks since you've exercised with the sword," he reminds me. "But now that your confinement is over, it is time for your practice to resume."

Carduc digs in the ground, then hands me the sword. It is heavy. My arms have grown weak so quickly.

"Your strength will return," Carduc promises.

It is good to hold the sword, to remember my defiance and my vow. "I will love no one but Tallas."

When Carduc first came, I worried that Prasutagus would return from the village and find me with the sword. Then I came to relish the fear; in my mind I saw Prasutagus come home, saw him stand at the doorway of our room, saw me turn to face him. Turn and smile. This is your wife. This is your wife and her sword.

My arms already strain. Prasutagus is not the husband of my heart. I do not love him, will not love him. I lie next to him at night, smile when a smile is demanded, and when he leaves the house, I dig up my father's sword, threaten his kingship with my defiance, strengthen my arms, honor my father and Tallas, remember what it is to be Iceni. It is good to remember.

"Just hold it today," Carduc instructs, "straight out in front of you for as long as you can."

He knows I will try to please him. "Watch over her," my father said before he drank the poison. "Yes," Carduc answered. That is what I imagine when I think of my father dying, except for the times when I see him calling me. "Boudicca." But I did not go to him. "Boudicca, why did you betray me?"

I did not betray you, Father.

The weight of the sword pulls my muscles taut–arms and shoulders, back and chest, stomach and legs. Longer. I'll hold it, longer.

Carduc responds to my grunt. "Don't strain. Put it down."

"A moment longer."

"Put it down."

Yes.

"Straining can bring on bleeding so soon after the child's birth. Don't do more than you can do now."

The child is Tallas's. The king's daughter is not the king's. The king must know, but he says nothing. But soon her face will show him. He is a king whose queen can look into her daughter's face to find her lover.

Carduc buries the sword again, then pulls the mat over the hiding place. So obvious, it seems. How could Prasutagus not know? How could he not want to kick the mat aside? "Is there anything under this mat? Is there a sword buried in the ground under this mat?" How could he not ask?

"Rest," Carduc advises, and then he is gone to wherever he goes. A work hut in the woods that Prasutagus bought permission for, though, after the disarming, no one was to have a hut beyond the Roman fort which bounds the village. But for the right price... These veterans left to guard us are not scrupulous. And Prasutagus is just as glad to have Carduc out of his sight having decided that in his need to distinguish himself from my father, he would not seek or accept Carduc's counsel. No, he is not my father.

But I do not want to rest. I want to hold my baby, Grawnei, study her. I want to see her face when it changes to Tallas's. See the lips when a flicker moves them into the shape of his mouth. See the eyes when they claim a color. Blue or green. Or both. See the place in her that knows him. Whisper his name to her. Tallas.

SEVEN

53 A.D.

"Send him in."

"Let me fix your hair first," Katha urges me.

It is a relief to feel the perspiration-sticky strands peeling away from the skin of my neck and my face. With a few quick movements, she coils it in the Roman fashion, then dunks a cloth into a bucket of cool water and wipes me down.

"An easier delivery than the first," she remarks. "Quicker."

"Not easy."

"No." She smiles. "Most aren't. Here." She offers to replace my torque around my neck.

"Not yet." I can still feel its fingers tightening at my throat, my neck straining against it before I tore it off. "Let me breathe a little more. Bring him in." I am anxious to please him with his new daughter.

"A girl," Katha announces when she opens the door to him.

He comes to my bed and stands until I invite him to sit beside me. He looks tired, worried. "How are you?"

"I'm well. This was an easier birth than the first." Katha and I smile to each other.

"I worried," he admits. "I thought of your mother..."

"It's over," I assure him. "I'm fine." I show him the bundle that Katha has made of the baby. "A girl," I repeat.

He takes her, disturbing the calm that is just coming over her. But he doesn't force her back on me when she cries. Instead, he gives her the tip of his finger, and she holds it in her mouth, teaching herself to suck.

A good father.

"Neidriu." I tell him her name.

He nods.

"Grawnei will be happy for a sister. Where is she? Does she want to come in?"

"She's outside with Carduc." He reflects for a moment. "She has a fascination for him."

I did too, when I was a child. But I'm sorry for Prasutagus's sense of exclusion, and to encourage him I say, "She has a fascination for you, too. I've seen her watch you when you're not looking."

"Have you?"

"Yes. And I've seen you watch her."

He smiles. "Yes, I suppose I do watch her, trying to learn something about her. She's so reticent a child."

"A brooder," Katha interjects.

Prasutagus smiles. "Sometimes I think she doesn't want me to know her."

"She's independent. And a thinker. And a bit of a loner, as well," I answer.

"Not much of a talker," he observes.

"No. But you can draw her out, Prasutagus. Your gentle way with her is just what she needs."

"She seems to prefer Carduc."

"When he's here, he lets her watch him work. She likes to watch, and she doesn't mind letting Carduc see her watch. With you, she's shyer. She watches, but she doesn't want you to see her watching."

"Why should she be shy with her father?"

We look directly at each other. You are not her father. He knows that; I think he knows. But maybe not; he never saw Tallas's eyes to know that Grawnei has them–blue, then green. Maybe he thinks she was an early baby, eight months instead of nine. "She has your brilliant hair," he has said, and "strange, changeable eyes." But he has never asked, "Whose eyes are those that she has?" He has never accused me. "She's young," I say, "but she senses your power. I think as she grows up, she'll always regard you as king first, then father."

He looks down at the baby. "And this one?"

This one is yours, I almost blurt. This one is the product of your persistent gentleness, and my weakness. I am your wife. I have given myself to you. "This one," I answer, "will have her own ways, too."

"You should rest now," Katha interrupts, and outstretches her arms for the baby. Prasutagus lays her there and stands to go.

"Don't leave yet," I request. "Stay a little longer. I want you by me until I fall asleep."

"I'll stay then."

Gentle man. Husband. Prasutagus.

Part Two

EIGHT

61 A.D.

"The king had two daughters," Neidriu begins, and she glances to Grawnei. "And he had a wife, the queen."

She smiles at me. And if Katha comes into the room, she will add her to the story so as not to hurt Katha's feelings by excluding her. And if Carduc comes in, she would give Carduc a part. Sensitive child.

"The king was very kind and generous," she continues, "and he never treated anyone harshly. All the people loved him. But then one day he became ill. Not very ill, but a little ill. And his daughters prayed to the gods to make him better. One daughter prayed very, very hard." She glances again to Grawnei. "No, both daughters prayed hard. And the gods said, 'Your father is a good king. Has he been praying to us, too?'"

She is worried that somehow Prasutagus has offended the gods, and they have sent illness as a punishment; she sees it as her duty to remind him to worship.

"And the daughters said, 'Yes, he has been praying, but he's a little weak so he's praying quietly.' And the gods said, 'Well, then, he will get better.' And he did get better." She smiles at the happy ending.

Prasutagus reaches for her. "He was a very lucky king to have such good daughters."

"We're the daughters," Neidriu reveals, excitedly.

Prasutagus pretends to be perplexed. "It's a story about us?"

"Yes," Neidriu squeals.

45

"Oh. I see. Yes. Two wonderful daughters and a lovely queen. Yes, it is about us, isn't it?"

"And a king who gets better," Neidriu reminds him.

"Yes, well, do you know what? I think your story worked. I do feel better."

"The prayers worked, father. The prayers."

Every day she offers something to the gods. Reverent child.

"The prayers worked," he agrees. "But the story helped, too. You're quite a storyteller."

"I like stories."

He laughs weakly. "Oh, I know you do. You've had me tell you every story I know."

"And Mother, and Katha and Carduc," she giggles. "They tell me stories, too."

"Well, then you must know every story ever told."

She considers this. "I think I do. But I forget them, too."

"That's why she likes to hear them over and over," I add. "Isn't it?"

She nods. "Can you tell me one now?"

"Your father has to rest."

"Just one. The one about the Roman emperor and his el. . ., his elfans . . . What were they called?"

"His elephants," Grawnei, who has been sitting quietly on the floor, instructs her.

"How do you know?" Neidriu asks.

"Carduc told me, and I remember."

"That's right." Prasutagus smiles at Grawnei. "Elephants. The emperor came to our land to show us his elephants."

"The emperor Claudius." Grawnei remembers the tale.

"Claudius," Prasutagus agrees.

"No one had seen an elephant before," Grawnei reminds him.

"And the elephants were very big." Neidriu stretches her arms out.

"Your mother's father saw the elephants," Prasutagus says.

"Did he, mother?" Neidriu turns eager eyes to me.

When he swore allegiance to Rome. "I saw the elephants, too."

46

"Did you?" Prasutagus asks, surprised.

"Didn't I ever tell you that?"

"Did you really see them, Mother? What were they like?" Neidriu demands.

They were majestic; I thought so then. Eleven kings gathered to swear loyalty to Rome, Rome in the person of Claudius, and he brought his elephants and his army to show us his might. I was awed, as all of us were meant to be. And I was proud of my father as he stood among the other kings and promised fealty to Claudius. I was proud. He was relinquishing his power, and I was proud. "I was quite young," I say, uneasy with the sudden reminder of my father at Rome's hand, of the raging hatred I once had for Rome, should still have but can no longer muster. But there is still a spark in me. But what good does hatred do me? It has never changed anything, and never will. I douse the spark with a deep sigh. "They were as tall as three oxen standing on one another's backs," I answer Neidriu. "And as wide as two wagons side by side."

"Were you scared?" she asks.

"I watched my father, and he didn't seem afraid, at least he didn't show any fear, so I wouldn't show mine. What made you want to hear about that now?"

"I don't know."

"Do you like that story, Grawnei?" Unlike Neidriu who would sit by her father's bedside day and night until he recovered, Grawnei is uncomfortable at having to bear witness to her father's sickness, and would rather be away from him, in the fields with the ponies and with her friends.

She shrugs.

"What is your favorite story?" I ask.

She considers. "I like the story of Vercingetorix."

"Vercingetorix?" I haven't thought of the story in so long.

"Where did you hear of Vercingetorix?" Prasutagus asks.

"From Carduc."

I nod, not surprised. "I remember the story of Vercingetorix. What did Carduc tell you about him?" I ask.

"Boudicca," Prasutagus warns me.

47

"Shh. It's all right," I assure him. "We all knew the story once. We were all told of Vercingetorix."

Grawnei begins. "Vercingetorix was a great king who lived across the sea."

She would end there if I did not prod her, so reticent and hesitant is she, even with her own family. "Go on."

"His people loved him. But then Rome came and tried to take his land. He fought them, and Rome tried to capture him. But he ran away."

"Rome wanted to help him and his people," Prasutagus instructs. "Rome was good to his people the way they have been good to us."

I do not contradict him, not aloud.

"But they killed him," Grawnei reminds Prasutagus. "They weren't good to him."

"He ran from Rome in fear when Rome only intended to help," Prasutagus answers sharply.

Now I can't restrain myself. "Prasutagus," I scold him. But he interrupts me before I can argue that Vercingetorix was not a coward. He knows that; I shouldn't have to remind him. He knew it once. He must have known it once. We all knew it. Didn't we?

"Rome intended to help, and he ran away, abandoning his people. That is all she needs to know of Vercingetorix," he says sternly. Then to Grawnei, "Do you understand?"

She hangs her head, chided, but does not answer.

"And I do not want you spending so much time with Carduc," Prasutagus instructs.

She will not look at him.

"Go, now," I dismiss her. "Your father needs to rest. Both of you, go and see if Katha needs help. Kiss your father."

"I love you, Father." Neidriu offers this pleadingly, upset that her father's peace has been disturbed. "Did you like the story *I* told?"

Always fretting, this child. Even as a baby she was nervous, difficult to calm. So fragile in her heart, and yet, bodily, so sturdy; she has never been ill. "Your father enjoyed your story," I assure her.

"Yes, very much," he assents.

But these assurances hardly comfort her, and once they leave the room she will surely chastise Grawnei for angering their father. Then the poor child will suffer because she hurt Grawnei's feelings, and all day she will make offerings to the gods.

Grawnei wouldn't kiss him if she had her way, not because he has spoken so firmly to her but because she feels an impropriety in this intimacy with his illness. As king, he should be strong, and that is how she wants to see him. King, first. Then father. But she obeys and brushes her lips against his cheek.

"I don't like the stories Carduc tells her," Prasutagus complains after the girls have left the room. "And if she goes out and repeats these stories to her friends..."

"She doesn't repeat them."

"How can you be sure?"

I don't answer.

"What do you think Flavinus would do if he discovered that my daughter was telling stories of rebels? My daughter, the king's daugh-ter–and only a king as long as I do Rome's bidding–telling stories of rebels? What if she told these stories to Flavinus's son when he visited? The king's daughter telling stories of rebels to the son of the garrison leader."

"Prasutagus, you're upsetting yourself over nothing. Lie back. Grawnei would never speak to Marcus of rebels. You know how taci-turn she is. Even with her friends. And Marcus, I'm afraid, is not one of her friends. She doesn't enjoy his company, and is happy now that he has returned to his mother in Rome. The match between them that you hoped for is not one Grawnei will want."

"I never proposed a match," he argues. "She's too young, yet. She's only a child."

"Yes, she's too young. And I know you would never force a mar-riage on her." Our eyes hold each other's for a long moment as he reads my message, my reminder to him that this marriage, though a happy one now, was not the marriage of my choice.

"I didn't want a marriage for them. Just a friendship."

But I know he had hoped. An offering to Rome. To peace. To friendship. But she will not be an offering. Not Tallas's daughter. "It will be Grawnei's choice when the time comes. That is the Iceni way."

"Yes," he agrees. "Of course. I would never force her."

"I know you wouldn't." I know he wouldn't. He is not cruel.

Irritable, now that I have exposed his secret hope for a match and deflated it, he asks, "Why has that old man taken such an interest in her, anyway?"

I know why. Carduc took his interest in her because he lost his interest in me when I stopped practicing with the sword, years ago, now. And I lost interest in him, and in his stories, and in the tiring, monotonous, meaningless practicing. But Grawnei has always been fascinated by him and has always followed him around. When I was still practicing, Carduc and I worried that she would seek him out when he was giving me lessons, find me holding the sword. Now, an alarming thought occurs to me. He might be teaching her the sword. What is this old man up to? "I'll limit their time together," I assure Prasutagus.

"Remind him that I was the one who brought him here. I was the one who bargained for permission for him to work in the woods. And he will do as I say, and respect me and respect Rome if he expects any privileges at all. He's of no use to me. Remind him of that, as well. What wisdom he once had he surely doesn't make known to me. I don't know how your father could have relied on him for counsel."

"He was wise," I say, "at one time. Now rest. Lie back. Shh."

But I must admit that I have no use for Carduc, now, either, and am happiest when he is away in the woods. Since I have refused to practice, he seems to have only disdain for me. But what was the use of sneaking around with a sword? What did I gain from it? The same that I gained from my hatred. Nothing. The strength I developed dissipated quickly- -a fleeting thing, strength. And why did I want to continue to betray Prasutagus in such a way when he had been so kind and so patient? Why should I have to listen to Carduc tell me over and over about how I honored my father and Tallas with the sword when Tallas and my father are gone and have been gone for so long? Why should I hold so fiercely to that life when that life brought such anguish? And my daughters. I had daughters to care for. "No," I told him. "Not today." Then again, "Not today." I was tired; an arm hurt; Neidriu or Grawnei was ill. Excuses. And then finally, "No, Carduc, I do not want you to come to me anymore. I will not work with the sword again."

I am weak. I know I am weak. I have let myself forget the anguish and the hatred. I am content. Almost content. Is it so bad to be content? There is peace. No border wars; no battle deaths. And Rome has been generous. Loans have been offered to all who want them by Seneca, one of their worthiest citizens–offering his own money, making it available for the asking. Breeders were bought, herds started. Can't we have anything we want? Carduc's iron ingots are so much easier to purchase now, right here at the market. And when he needs more, isn't he allowed to travel west to make his trade? Why shouldn't I be content? Why can't Carduc? Why should I keep deceiving Prasutagus, keep daring Rome with my sword? Why should I pretend for Carduc that I do not love Prasutagus? My husband. My husband whom Carduc sent me to insisting on dignity from me. I love him. I have broken vows, and I am weak, but I love him.

So now Carduc tells Grawnei stories. Does he think she will give him what I do not? And what does he want? To keep the ways alive? There are no ways. No ways that matter. Only stories. Stories that Carduc told me, too. That Tallas told me. Vercingetorix. Who fought Rome then eluded them when they sought him. Vercingetorix, who handed himself over when he heard of the abuses Rome was meting out to his people in his name. "The Romans stood awed," Carduc had said, Tallas, too, "when they saw the majesty of him–his height, his flowing, flaming hair and moustache, his blatant strength." A king. But Rome does not stand in awe of anything for long, anything that is not itself, and Vercingetorix was chained and paraded through the village and the countryside for all to see his shame. "But the chains could not diminish his stature," Tallas said. "And everywhere he went, he walked straight and people cheered." Yes, and then when Rome grew bored of the spectacle, they imprisoned him, let him wither for years, then cut off his head and paraded him again.

I remember the story. The stories. Prasutagus remembers, too. But now he tells them as he must, in the Roman way, to protect his family, protect himself.

I wipe his face with a cool cloth.

Husband.

"Shh. Rest. So Grawnei knows a story. It's only a story. An old story. Shh."

NINE

"Have you shown her the sword, Carduc?"

"The sword is yours."

"Have you shown her?"

"No."

"Don't." My gaze is steady. "What do you teach her?"

"How to work iron, the way I showed you when you were young."

"You showed me how to work iron into a sword." He doesn't reply. "What do you show her now that you no longer mold swords?"

"Tools. Spearheads."

"Daggers?"

"I've shown her how to mold a dagger."

"And you tell her stories?"

"Our stories. Stories she should be told."

"Of Vercingetorix?" I ask.

"Of Vercingetorix."

"And Caratacus?" He asked for mercy. And is alive in Rome. A citizen.

"Caratacus. Before he was made a Roman."

"Tallas?" I ask, forcing my gaze to hold its steadiness.

"That's for you to tell," he says.

"Yes." I used to whisper his name to her. But when she learned how to talk, I stopped.

Carduc sees me remember. "You used to tell her stories. I heard you. What stories do you tell her now? And her sister? Stories of the greatness of Rome?" It is an accusation.

"I tell them of the gods," I defend myself. "And of my father. And of my mother."

"You never knew your mother."

"I tell them anyway. And it isn't for you to say which stories I may tell my children. It is for me to say. And I don't want you telling her any more stories. She'll learn what she needs to know from Prasutagus and me."

Another accusing question is on his lips. "Will she?" I can see him start to form it. But he doesn't ask, instead, he nods and obliges. "When she comes to me I will send her to you. I will tell her that her mother can teach her everything she needs to know." He pauses. "It is the truth. You could teach her, if you would."

TEN

His illness resists all herbs, all poultices. Prasutagus is dying.

If he asks me to kill him, I will, with poison or a dagger thrust. Poison; I could not force a dagger into his chest. Poison, and Carduc would have to prepare it as he prepared my father's. The council would have to question me as is their duty, but it is my right. Mercy, not murder. And to kill in mercy is no crime. But he does not ask. I believe he is afraid to die.

"Boudicca," he rasps.

"I'm here."

"I dreamed of you again."

"Did you?"

"I dreamed of you in the stream. Your hair floated on the surface, all around you. And I was there, grabbing onto your hair."

"Shh."

"Will you make me a bracelet? A few strands of your hair so that you will accompany me in some way to the next life."

"Prasutagus."

"Please."

"You'll get better." I try to reassure him, though I don't believe it.

"Boudicca." He struggles to sit up in the bed. His arms can hardly support his weight. "Will you promise me the bracelet?"

"I promise."

"Have you wondered what will happen when I die?" he asks gently.

I have. I have been thinking about it with more and more frequency.

"Are you worried?"

"Yes," I admit.

"Tell me."

My concerns are selfish; I hesitate.

"Tell me," he repeats.

"It is my right as your wife to succeed you, but Rome will not name me."

"No."

I had still imagined that there might be a possibility. But no, I knew there wasn't. "Whom will they name?"

"Garan, possibly. I believe they'll choose from among the council, and he has been a member since I was named king. He has always been admiring of Rome. Flavinus trusts him, and as garrison leader, it will be Flavinus's duty to make a recommendation to the governor, Paulinus. Then Paulinus will decide. As long as the tribute is collected, Rome will be satisfied."

Still, my salient concern is not addressed, and yet I hesitate to ask.

Prasutagus reads the lingering perturbation in my face. "You'll be provided for," he offers.

"That's not what worries me."

"What, then?"

"Garan..." I begin, faltering, "and Rome."

"In what way?"

"Prasutagus," I don't want to upset him, "forgive me, but...I worry about another marriage being forced on me. I don't want to marry again." There. I am glad to have said it. The thought of it has made me anxious for weeks; when my attention should have been on my husband, it has been on myself.

He smiles sadly. "Was this so bad for you?"

I take his hand. "No, though I wanted it to be." I look away from his face to the hand that I hold. "You were not my choice."

"No. But then it is childish to believe all of our choices could be honored."

"I suppose it is."

He fixes his gaze on the fire.

Tallas. My choice. He still stirs in me. And in Prasutagus, what is stirring in him? What is he seeing in the flame that brings such a look of loss to his face? A choice? A choice he didn't make, couldn't make? Was I not his choice? I never thought of him as being denied a choice. I only thought of him as an agent of Rome's desire, not a pawn of Rome, as I was. But it is possible...I was not his choice. Yet, he could have taken a second wife, the one who was his choice. Though perhaps not. Perhaps Rome wanted him to stand as an example of their monogamy. Who was she whom he wanted?

"Perhaps," I begin tentatively, "it is I who should ask, 'has it been so bad for you?'"

He lets go of what held him in the flames, and smiles. "No, not so bad."

We sit silently for several moments. It stings me that I was not his choice. As unfair as that feeling is, since I did not want him, it still hurts me, embarrasses me.

"You bore the duty of our marriage well," I quietly commend him.

"And you, too," he grants me, and smiles, knowing, as I do, that his dignity in this greatly surpassed mine, at least in our first few years together. And I am ashamed for my childishness, my selfishness, my conviction that I, alone, suffered in this marriage.

He continues, "I don't think Rome will force another marriage on you. You have proved yourself to be trustworthy and reasonable. They do not consider you a threat anymore; certainly they don't see you as a possible instigator of a rebellion as they once did. My concern would be that Garan or whoever was named would want to increase his wealth and his land holdings through a marriage to you. Garan is an ambitious man. If he requested such a marriage, Rome might agree to it, and order it. But I have thought of that already, too, and have already notified Flavinus of the arrangement I have decided on for the land." He continues, "At my death, one- third of our land and our wealth will be granted to the emperor, Nero. I will give him the property that was your father's."

An instinct makes me want to fight for what was my father's. "You give my father's land away so easily."

Now he begins to sink back into the bed, the little strength he had summoned, exhausted. "That land is apart from this. Would you rather share the land here and live side by side with Rome? A portion of the land should be handed over. This is the best arrangement. Nero will see the goodwill in this act. It will dispose him favorably to you. Your father would have approved; like me, he sought ways to maintain peace. The other two-thirds will be divided between our daughters. You will manage it for them until they are old enough, then they will provide for you. A marriage to you will yield nothing, as you own nothing, and a marriage to one of our daughters would only yield a third of the land. Garan would not dishonor himself or risk the disfavor of the gods and the tribe by taking a child-wife for the sake of just a third of my land. Does that put you at ease?"

"Thank you."

"Now, come, lie down next to me. I need to sleep, and I want you with me."

I am reassured, but now with Prasutagus's plan articulated to me, the future–his death–is brought nearer. His body, next to mine, feels so frail. I close my eyes and see what will come: he is lifeless on our bed; Neidriu and Grawnei weep; I weep.

ELEVEN

Before dawn I am awakened, not by a sound, but by a presence I sense in the room.

Sitting up, I speak into the darkness, "Who is it? Who's there?" Strands of my hair have become entangled in Prasutagus's fingers–he grasps for it during the night–and now I have to tug it, break some of the strands to free myself.

"Did you hear cries as you slept?" a voice questions.

"Grawnei? Neidriu? Are they ill?" I ask. "Carduc? Is that you?"

"Your children are safe for now, though I fear none of us will be safe again."

"Speak plainly, Carduc," I whisper sharply. "Do you have some news?"

"What is it?" Prasutagus asks, waking now. "Who is that?"

"It is Carduc," he announces himself.

"You enter without permission?"

"He has news that he presents in a riddle," I charge.

"What is the news?" Prasutagus demands.

"Seutonius Paulinus has attacked Mona, the island of the priests."

"The Druids?" Prasutagus asks, straining to see Carduc.

"Yes. Nothing is left alive–not man, or woman, or child. Even the sacred groves have been hacked and burned. In their frenzy and their fear, the Romans laid the island barren. The keepers of the sacred knowledge are dead," he laments. "The knowledge is lost. For the

59

Iceni, and for all the tribes of Britain, the ancient wisdom is lost. For generations the Druids have studied the land and the sky and learned what pleases the gods and displeases them. They have made our law, and settled our disputes, and healed when no one else could. Now they are dead, and the knowledge dies with them. The teachings cannot be passed down. The next generations will never know our ways."

From outside the room, a guard calls to Prasutagus.

"Do you have news of Mona?" Prasutagus asks.

"It has been attacked."

"Enter."

"What else do you know?" Prasutagus asks.

"The priests are dead. And Romans soldiers are in the village now, preventing anyone from assembling. A troop from Camulodumnum is on the way," the guard answers.

"We are to accept this atrocity without a response," Carduc interprets the guard's news. "Paulinus has long wanted to make a reputation for himself," he says, "the way Scapula made his reputation on Caratacus years ago."

And on Tallas.

"Mona is rich with copper; Paulinus wanted it. But more than that, he wanted the priests dead because they spoke so openly against Rome and provided refuge for any of Rome's enemies who sought it."

"Did anyone escape? Did they offer resistance?" I ask.

"The priests do not arm themselves," he reminds me impatiently, even condescendingly, as if I have forgotten everything I was once taught. "The only ones who survived are those who were not on the island."

"I know the priests do not carry weapons, Carduc. But didn't they get assistance from anyone else? None of the western tribes..."

"No one was prepared. No one believed Paulinus would dare attack the island. I've heard the priests lined the shores, arms linked, naked and chanting, while the order of black-cloaked women who lived among them shrieked madly, throwing themselves to the ground, jumping up again. Some torched their hair and their cloaks, burning themselves alive for the sake of prostrating Rome with horror. Paulinus hesitated, but his pride proved greater than his fear. He forced his men into the straits of Menai; they crossed in flat-bottomed boats, thousands of them, horsemen too, and the priests could only watch them come." He is silent then, as if wanting to give us time to imagine this scene and know the terror, and I do.

Turning to me, Prasutagus asks for help dressing. "We will go into the village and meet the Roman troop, and calm the villagers."

I assist him, though my hands tremble. "Paulinus must be mad," I say. Where would he turn that madness next? I guide Prasutagus's legs into one pair of wide bracae, then another, direct his arms into one tunic, and another, then a third. We do this, not only to keep the chill away–he is so susceptible to chills–but so that his frailty will be hidden beneath the layering of clothing. Over his shoulders I swing his heaviest cloak, though he sags with the weight of it. I dress quickly.

Katha is already at the hearth, weepy and jumpy and red-nosed from crying, but no less efficient, handing us cakes that I take and Prasutagus refuses.

"Keep the children close," I instruct her.

Carduc has readied the chariot. But Prasutagus calls for our riding horses. He does not trust his legs; they may give out as he stands on the platform of the chariot. The horse will hold his weight for him, if he can just sit.

Accompanied by six guards, we ride slowly into the village, past rows of huts laid out with Roman precision. I am anxious, and jump at the call of a crow. "Do you think they are planning on murdering all of us?"

Prasutagus does not answer.

But that is not my only fear. The gods are surely greatly offended by this blasphemous act and will soon have their retaliation. The air itself bristles with their anger.

At the marketplace, merchants have already gathered but are being prevented from setting up their stands by Roman soldiers who are instructing them to return to their homes. Among the soldiers is Flavinus. His demeanor now with Prasutagus is not the one we are used to, not the one he presented just a few weeks ago when we dined together as friends before Prasutagus became ill. Instead of the warmth we are used to from him, he offers us imperiousness.

"The Iceni are to remain in their homes," he demands. "Have that order sent out." Prasutagus nods. And then as though he remembers their friendship, Flavinus lets his voice take on concern. "A troop has been deployed from Camulodumnum. They will be quick to use their swords." Again, my husband nods, understanding the warning. Mona is not mentioned.

The Romans must be as afraid of the gods' vengeance as we are. Insist, as they will, that they do not believe in our gods, they fear them nevertheless, and know this act will bring their wrath. Yes, their fear will make them quick with their swords.

We turn and ride silently, perhaps wondering over the same questions: did Flavinus know? Was he aware all along of Paulinus's plan? When he dined with us as a friend, did he know the priests were to be murdered?

The gods will have revenge. The Druids will have revenge. This night air is a thin veil, beneath it the spirits of the otherworld are gathering. That is this awful chill.

Prasutagus directs us down an alley of huts, orders the guards to dismount, and has them rap at several of the doors. When a resident has appeared in each doorway, he announces, "Rome has invaded Mona. Remain at home. Prepare offerings to the gods. A Roman troop is on its way here to guard against any retaliatory action by us. They have orders to kill anyone who is about." He makes several such stops, calling up a strength that surprises me. At each stop he asks for assistance in spreading the word, and soon the various cries of alarm float in an unbroken gasp through the dark village.

I feel watched. The old sensation. And as we ride, I move my eyes in every direction.

Even at home I suspect a presence and move restlessly from room to room. For the rest of the morning Prasutagus rests near the hearth with a blanket over his shoulders. Neidriu and Grawnei, though happy to see him up, are aware that the occasion is not a celebratory one and sit quietly, waiting for an opportunity to arrange his blanket, fill his soup bowl. Even Grawnei wants to offer help, offer a touch to her father, smooth the fretful forehead which worries her.

At night the sleeping is fitful for everyone; several times Neidriu calls out for me.

In the morning we ride into the village again. Prasutagus requests permission for a mass sacrifice to appease the gods and the spirits of the Druids. Flavinus denies the request, informing him that no one is to leave their home until the troop has arrived from Camulodumnum, and that after that, assemblies of more than two people will be forbidden. Those found in larger groups will be arrested on a charge of conspiring revenge.

Prasutagus sends messengers throughout the village with the warning, and suggests that offerings be made individually.

Later, in our yard, we kill a cow and a goat and set their carcasses on fire.

The troop arrives on the second day, and on the third, the market is allowed to reopen. The strength that Prasutagus has rallied over the last few days is remarkable, but tenuous. Still, he travels into the village again. The soldiers from Camulodumnum, many of whom are veterans who chafe in the uniforms they have outgrown with their indulgent ways, crowd the marketplace, urging the few Iceni who have ventured out only out of necessity to move quickly and refrain from conversation. Flavinus greets us, escorts us to the south end of the marketplace where an open tent has been set up. Inside, behind a table, sits Procurator Catus Decianus, a tribute collector with whom we have had acquaintance before. With him is his companion, a young boy of Grawnei's age.

"Dismount," Flavinus instructs us. I hesitate on two counts. I fear that Prasutagus will need assistance, and I do not want to announce his weakness by offering it. Further, it is an insult to ask a king to dismount for the sake of a greeting. But Flavinus clearly means to diminish my husband's authority. Prasutagus slowly obliges. When he is standing alongside his horse, he nods to me, and I dismount, as well. We are greeted by Decianus.

"As you know," he begins, "large sums of money have been loaned to your people. To artisans for supplies, villagers so they could purchase some of the goods sent by Rome, others who wanted to start a herd of their own–all have had willing assistance from our generous and wise citizen, the philosopher Seneca. Now," Decianus continues, "it is his wish to call in those loans."

"Call in the loans?" Prasutagus asks. "All of them, for the full amount?"

"All of them. In full," Catus Decianus answers sternly.

"How do you expect people to pay such amounts on such short notice?" Prasutagus asks.

"How they do it is not our concern," Flavinus joins in in the officious tone with which he greeted us the day before. "What is our concern, and yours, is that they do. We've sent messengers. Send your own as well. Tell those who owe that the debt is to be repaid. If they cannot pay in Roman money, they will pay in goods or in land. Or labor. Those who cannot make payment will become the property of Seneca. And in his generosity to Rome, he has granted us the freedom to use these debtors as we will. Catus Decianus has the log books here," he continues. "See to it that those whose names are included in it appear to him over the next days to make arrangements." Flavinus had not dismounted, and now he pulls on his horse's reins and turns away.

Prasutagus does not examine the log book that Decianus holds out for him. He remounts, swinging his leg over slowly, but surely, and sits erect. I quickly follow and we ride, at a trot, away from the procurator.

"It is their misgivings that force them to treat us so harshly," he says later when we are home at the hearth and he has been deliberating over this stunning change in treatment. "They are afraid of what Paulinus did. And they are afraid of reprisals from us, from the gods, and from the spirits of the Druids. They need now to subdue us, to show us their power, to make us afraid because in their hearts they fear us now as much as we fear them. And that fear makes them dangerous."

But Rome has always been dangerous, I want to remind him. It has only been for the sake of our comfort that we have pretended that it wasn't.

That night, Prasutagus sleeps heavily, and in the morning awakens but only groggily, and then, sleeps again. The day passes slowly. Grawnei wants the company of the horses, but I won't let her out to the fields. Neidriu clings to me. When night comes again, I find our bed unwelcoming. Death is there. I can feel it–Prasutagus's companion now. He mumbles to it.

TWELVE

From the underlayers of my hair, I cut a certain thickness. It is darker than the russet top layers that Prasutagus knows, but it will satisfy his desire. When I've braided it carefully and tied it at each end, I wrap it around his wrist. If he wakes again, he will find it there and know that I've kept my promise.

And what will this promise bring me? Will it direct him to me in our next lives? Make me his again? Would it be so terrible to be his again? This time, though, as a choice–not a mandate. A choice. Would I choose him?

As soon as she is up and dressed, Neidriu makes her offering. Each day she throws a handful of grain, a cake, a bit of clay she's molded in a special way, something into the hearth fire and asks the gods to protect us. I believe that if she knew of the orders of women who devote themselves to the gods she would want to join them, except that she would have to live away from home and that would be unbearable for her. Today she is not satisfied with her offering.

"Do you think the gods are angry?" She worries.

"Yes," I tell her honestly.

"And sad?"

"Yes, and sad."

She thinks for a moment, then decides, "We should walk a blessing on the house."

"That's a good idea. Go and get your sister."

Once in the yard, the three of us, holding hands, start around the house in a sun-wise direction. With her free hand, Neidriu sifts grain through her fingers and sprinkles the softening ground with it. "Protect our house," she chants. "Protect our house."

Grawnei watches her sister intently, more interested in the reverence she exhibits, the fervor, than in the offering. We walk the house three times. Each time, instead of gaining potency, the prayers feel more and more insufficient, and a sense of dread, rather than of protection seems to gather around us. The Druids are dead. The Druids, who knew best how to appease the gods, cannot protect us. The girls sense it too, and draw closer to me as we make our last circuit. Though I'm sure she'd rather cling to me, Neidriu sacrifices her own comfort and offers to spend the rest of the morning at her father's bedside, praying–no doubt imploring–the gods to forgive, to protect. Grawnei surprises me by saying that she will join her sister, though she will likely do her praying a safe distance from the bed.

All morning I am uneasy, as though I am waiting, as though my body knows something is to happen before my mind knows what that will be. I walk from room to room, thankful for the space to wander. This home, like my father's, is larger than the typical Iceni one-roomed circular hut. With our hearth room at the center and short passageways extending on the north and the south ends of that central room to two other rooms on each side, I have a fair amount of space to give over to my restlessness. In one room I finger the loom, but cannot stop to sit at it; in another I walk the circumference of the table at which the council meets and where we entertain guests and have special meals. My hand runs over the backs of chairs. Back through the hearth room, I stop to help Katha wipe a spill of vinegar–turn my face from the sharp odor that I have always disliked. Down the other hallway I stand outside my room, listening to Neidriu speak soothingly to her father; she is telling another story of a king and his daughters, a strong threesome who provide for all of their people. Grawnei is silent. In my daughters' room, I take in the sweet smell of them and pray for their safety.

Later, at last, a messenger comes. Good news or bad, I must have some relief from the oppression of waiting that has confined me all morning. It is a message from Leth, one of Prasutagus's councilmen. He advises me that news of my husband's illness is spreading, and he suggests that I ride into the village.

"Seeing you," the messenger repeats Leth's words, "will give the people assurance that they will still have a leader when their king dies."

But I will not be their leader, and Leth must be able to surmise that. Still, he is right in knowing that the people need assurance. And it is my duty, at least until Prasutagus dies and a new king is named, to assume this role.

As I ride into the village, guards accompanying me, I witness several groups of Iceni being led away by Roman veterans. Debtors. Slaves, now, who will be brought to Camulodunum to be put to work on the temple and the system of roads Rome is building to link its colonies, east to west, north to south.

Within one of the processions I recognize Leanan whose husband, Coel, never returned to her after Tallas's rebellion. So tempting was Seneca's offer of loans that even those who could have done without them accepted the terms. She had other ways. She could have come to me and asked for the privilege of celsine, and I would have been happy to see to it that she was taken onto our land and protected, her tribute paid in exchange for light duties. But her pride would not allow her to ask, and I could not force her. Instead, she embraced indebtedness to Seneca. I believe the desire to trust him was as much a factor in accepting his offer as need was. A desire existed to embrace Rome as an ally. Seneca was Rome, and he wanted to see us prosper. How seductive that belief was–I remember I called him generous–and how perilous.

I approach the procurator, Catus Decianus. He is calling out names from his list, giving orders for those people to be brought to him. I see that he has already claimed several of the Iceni debtors for himself and has enlisted them to assist in his roundup of other debtors. Iceni forced to help turn Iceni over to Rome. I look over this group, recognize many of the faces, then quickly look away, not wanting to worsen their shame with my gaze.

I pay Decianus respect by dismounting my chariot. He repays me by continuing to call out names.

"What is the amount of Leanan's loan?" I interrupt him. "Leanan, whose mother was Anan and whose husband was Coel," I tell him, so that he can identify her by her family.

"Why?" He looks at me now. Dark eyes. Large mouth.

"I will pay it for her."

"Will you? Do you know what your people have been asking me?"

I do not answer.

"As a way of reneging on their debts, they are asking if they can postpone payment until their next lives." He laughs. "I understand it is a practice among you people to wriggle out of debts by promising to pay in your next incarnation."

Again, I say nothing. It is true: such arrangements have been made occasionally. For me, I would not want to enter my next life so indebted, but for some who cannot possibly repay their debts in this life but do not want dishonor to follow them into the next life, such an agreement can be made and sealed with an exchange of blood, wrist to wrist, as a way of being able to know one another in the next life.

"Do you know what I say to them?" Decianus asks. "I ask them how they can be sure they'll be able to pay in the next life. Because if they are sure, if they are planning on being rich in the next life, I'll kill them right now and hurry them into that life." He chortles, then looks at his journal. "Your friend owes forty sesterces."

It is a large sum; I doubt she borrowed so much. Surely Seneca charged high fees, and Decianus has probably added on some for himself.

I promise it and ask for her release.

"Would you buy freedom for just one of your people? Or shall I tell you the cost of buying it for all of them?" he taunts me.

"Leanan," I repeat, "and her sons."

"Her sons?" He checks his record. "Her sons have already been sent to Camulodumnum. Maybe onto Rome."

"Have them returned."

"When I receive payment, I will have them returned. If they can be found."

"You'll have payment this afternoon."

He turns to a guard. "Go," he commands. "Bring the woman, Leanan, here. Make sure the rest of them know that their queen has bought her release but will not buy release for the others."

I let out a sigh, watch what I hoped was a good deed become bad. I had come to offer reassurance, but now my people will see me abandon them.

"What else can I do for you today?" Decianus asks.

"That will be enough," I reply.

Leanan is brought to me. She looks about her suspiciously, and at me, accusingly. I take her onto my chariot, signal my guard to move, and we are hardly out of earshot of Decianus when she speaks to me, respectfully, but with anger. "I am grateful for your generosity. But you have separated me from my sons. I was happy to go as a slave to Camulodumnum. At least I could get a glimpse of my children and know they were safe."

Her boys are older than Grawnei—one by almost two years, the other by mere months. It is old enough for boys to know how to protect themselves, and yet I think of how afraid I would be for Grawnei if she were taken from me.

I assure her that I have demanded her sons' return. But the words don't comfort either of us. I ride slowly through the market—what there is of it—and offer encouragement, buy a new bowl for Katha, and some honey sticks for the girls, but feel the pretense of it, know it is a show, know it is seen as a show, and doubt its effectiveness in reassuring anyone.

In the silence of the ride home, I am thinking of the offers made to Catus Decianus to repay Seneca in later lives, and wondering: if spirits travel from body to body, from life to life as we know them to, then the Romans' spirits will travel, too. And does that mean they will be among us in the next life? Among us forever? Will we have to fear each life the gods give us?

At home I put Leanan in Katha's care; she in turn will put her in the care of one of the families on our land.

Neidriu and Grawnei have been steadfast in their vigil, and now I relieve them. There is a change in Prasutagus. The color of his face is a light ash, and he has passed into a state of open-mouthed, irregular breathing. It is his death sleep. I sit at the edge of the bed and take his cool hand in mine. I desperately want his company again, want him to wake up just one more time. "Just one more time, Prasutagus."

That night, I do not want to be in the bed when death comes; I sleep on blankets on the floor, on the mat under which the sword lies. There is a vague comfort in being so near to the sword. Though I haven't wanted it in years, I am glad for its company tonight.

In the morning, I call to Prasutagus, but I already know he won't answer. "Prasutagus." His forehead, when I brush the hair back, is cold. He is dead, and this body that was his is now empty, so clearly empty. Still, I want to be here with it for just one moment, just one more moment. "Prasutagus."

Neidriu comes into the room to greet him as she does each morning. "Father? Father?"

"He is gone, Neidriu."

"To the gods?" she asks hopefully, tearfully.

"To the gods," I assure her. "And on to his next life." One without Romans, I pray.

"He'll live again," she says as if to convince herself, and I believe she is imagining him as he is, as he was, waiting for her in the next life.

"Grawnei, would you like to come in?" She is standing outside the room. "No?" She remains there, and does not cry.

Katha and Carduc help me to groom and perfume him. I make sure that the hair I have cut and braided is secure at his wrist. Messengers are sent to the council members and to Flavinus with the news.

This is a strange time when Prasutagus is in the house, but not, when his body lies here emptied of its spirit but remains visibly still a husband, a father, and yet is completely disconnected from this world.

Flavinus comes to offer his sympathy and respect, but he has a bitter warning to deliver, also. The restriction on assembling is still in effect. The tribe may not attend Prasutagus's death ceremony. In fact, Flavinus instructs that the ceremony will be handled in the Roman way– Prasutagus's body is to be burned on a pyre here on our land. Though many of our people have accepted the Roman way of cremation, some of us still prefer the old method of burial. It is an outrage and an insult that Flavinus does not leave the choice to me, but he has brought armed guards to ensure I comply. I am reminded of Tallas's death and Scapula's threat to leave him unburied. Even their gods, gods of their own creation, will have to judge harshly these Romans who would dishonor a person at their death.

The pyre burns and burns. Neidriu tries to watch but her sobs are so violent that she will choke on them. I take her back to the house. Katha tends to her while I watch from the doorway as my husband's body becomes weightless smoke and ash, and rises toward the low sky. I can almost see his spirit fly, and that heartens me.

Our field workers and herd tenders watch the flames and the Roman guards from outside their huts. Grawnei stands by the pyre, honoring him now as the king that he was, offering, with her straight back and her stoic silence, the pride that she could not give him in his illness. She will have regrets. She will want to have treated him with more tenderness while he was sick. She will be telling him now in her silence that she is sorry. That she loved him. The way I told my father after his death that I was sorry.

THIRTEEN

Why do I think of Tallas? In the morning, when I awaken, Prasutagus is dead, and I think of Tallas. Still dead. I remember this painful waking each morning, remember knowing as I floated up from sleep, one thing: Tallas was dead. Now Prasutagus. And every morning, he will be dead. And yet, the pain, I must admit, is not as searing. I will not take to my bed; I do not wish to absent myself from this world the way I did when Tallas died. I will bear this death, and show my daughters how to bear it.

It is still early morning, and Neidriu is at the hearth with me, contemplating another offering when one of my guards anxiously announces that Catus Decianus, accompanied by a small but armed contingent of his men, is on his way to the house.

Leanan, whom Katha did not assign to one of our field families but befriended and made a guest, looks up from the cloak that she is mending. "Perhaps he is bringing my sons," she suggests.

"Perhaps. Still, as a precaution, I think you should stay out of his sight in case he has ideas of reclaiming you. Go to Lamerok. His hut is the one closest to the stables. Tell him I said you should stay there until I send for you." I do not believe Decianus is bringing her sons. Not accompanied by armed guards. I send Neidriu to her room and tell her to sit with her sister. "Where is Carduc?" I ask Katha. I would like him with us now.

"Out at the hut. Should I go get him?"

What am I so afraid of? "Yes, ask him to come in."

But it is too late. Decianus arrives. He enters with six guards. They stand in a line blocking the door.

I stand to greet him. "I sent payment yesterday," I tell him, trying to discern his intention. Perhaps he expected me to add to the amount--an extra payment for him, though I'm sure he included that in the price. "But if I owe you more, there are coins in the house..."

"I received payment," he says, taking a step toward me.

I hold myself in place though my body is urging me to back away, to run. "Did you bring Leanan's sons?" I inquire, feigning calm. I look past him to his guards. Where are *my* guards?

"Sons?" he repeats. "I'm here about daughters."

Daughters. That word in his mouth chills me. My daughters.

"I'm told your husband had some arrangement for the division of his land–your daughters and the emperor are expected to share it? Let me see these daughters."

"They are resting," I insist. "They are mourning the loss of their father."

"Let me see them," he demands. "Or shall I send my guards for them?"

I try to look past Decianus's men to my guards, but the door has been shut now, and my men closed out. I nod to Katha to bring the girls.

Catus Decianus laughs at the sight of them. "So, these are the beasts who are to share Nero's wealth?"

In a moment I am grabbed, my arms pinned behind me. Katha gasps and is struck in the face by Catus Decianus, then held by a soldier as I am. Neidriu cries out and rushes to me but Decianus snatches her before she reaches me.

"Neidriu." I am slapped. "Neidriu," and slapped again. "Grawnei, run." I am hit again. Grawnei is caught, her arms pinned, as mine are. The force the Roman soldier uses on her lifts her from the ground. She is carried from the room.

"Mother. Mother."

Decianus, raging, pushes Neidriu up against a wall. Her feet are in the air, and he pushes himself against her.

"Neidriu."

He is thrusting himself into her.

"Neidriu."

Her face is hidden by his mass. He thrusts. Her head hits the wall. A small moan is forced from her. Her foot shoots out. Left foot.

"Neidriu, I am here. I am here." Her foot shoots out. I am hit again. Her foot. Her foot. "Neidriu." Another slap. Another thrust. "Neidriu."

Then he stops. Her foot dangles, limp. He moves his weight off her, and she slides down the wall to the floor and slumps there.

"Neidriu." I struggle against the soldier who is holding me. "Let me go. Neidriu. Grawnei. Where is Grawnei?"

Decianus turns his attention to me. "A chair," he demands. "And a drink." Katha is pushed so that she falls, and then is kicked.

"Get up." The soldier kicks her again. "Bring wine."

She gets to her feet, hunching to protect the kicked spots, brings a chair, and, with trembling hands, pours a cupful of wine.

Decianus sits and drinks, and after a gulp, says, "Her tunic."

With a single, violent motion, thick hands tear a rip the full length of my garment. It is then stripped from me, and I am held there, naked.

Decianus smiles. "Did you dare to dishonor Nero by proposing that he share this property with two girls?" he asks as he gulps the wine that Katha has handed him. "Barbarian girls at that?"

I can barely steady my voice to speak. "Flavinus... approved of the arrangement," I murmur. Neidriu lies on the floor, her knees pulled to her chest, her hand pressing the soreness between her legs. Her tunic is dribbled with blood. She rocks. "Where is Flavinus?" I ask, my voice breaking.

"Flavinus is not here." Decianus stands. "Whip her."

The quick leather ignites my skin, but it is the heavy tip of the whip that bites deepest and lands last. I count to put my mind on something. Three, four, five, six. I think my legs are gone from under me.

The whipping stops. I am still standing; my legs haven't given. Decianus steps forward, grabs my breasts in his hands and squeezes me until tears run from my eyes.

"Your husband knew that this territory was to be annexed at his death. One-third to Rome, two-thirds to Rome, three-thirds to Rome. His 'arrangement' was a lie to you. Did he tell you you would be queen, too? Well then, let us honor the queen." I am whipped again.

I know nothing but the rhythm of pain–a burst like a flame and then heat, burst and heat, burst and heat. Burst. And heat. And heat. The bursts stop. A trick. When I open my eyes they'll start again. Keep your eyes closed, Boudicca. A burst. Boudicca. I drop. Raging heat. Boots on the floor. Scraping. Stomping. Keep your eyes closed. Boots. Heat. Are they leaving? Keep your eyes closed. Are they gone? Don't look. Don't move. Just a glimpse. Gone? Gone? Neidriu, I am coming. I'm coming.

"Be still," Katha warns.

I stop moving. Was I moving? "Neidriu."

"Shh."

"Neidriu."

"Be still."

"Are they gone? They are gone. Katha, they are gone." I crawl to Neidriu. Her body convulses. "I'm here. I'm here. It's over."

"Grawnei," Katha says hoarsely, "is in her room."

"Help me, Katha. Get her."

I am dying. I can feel my body letting go, my flesh burning away.

There are others, now. Carduc, and my guards, Leanan.

Then I am in my bed with Neidriu curled toward me, Grawnei curled away.

My skin still plays the rhythm of the pain. Burst and heat. Burst and heat. Burst and heat. My mind plays the rhythm, too, burst and heat.

FOURTEEN

Apollo-Belinus, Minerva, Taranis, Esus, Epona, Icena. Icena. How have we offended you? Why has this been brought on us? My daughters. Neidriu. She offers a handful of grain, a cake, her weaving. She offers something every day. Every day she asks for your blessing. Every day she praises you. Don't you see her when she walks us sun-wise around the house? Three times, asking for blessings. Then he comes and pounds her against the wall. How do you let this happen? Her foot, bouncing. Little foot. Innocent foot. I will never see a worse sight. If I saw her dead, it would not be as awful. I close my eyes, and it is still there. If burning my eyes would burn the sight away, I would put a flame to them. Do you want my eyes? I would give you my eyes if I could stop seeing it. But even in blindness, I would see it.

Prasutagus, did you see? Did you know? Did you know that Rome would come? Did you know we would be so horribly punished for your plan? Did you tell me just to put me at ease, all the while knowing Nero would reject it? And they would come. Did you know they would come? Your daughters. Your own daughters. Did you? You couldn't have known.

Her foot. His back. I can't see her face, can't meet her eyes and let her know that I am still there. Look at me, Neidriu. Look at me. I am here. It will be over, and I am here. No. I cannot tell her, cannot see her. Only his back. And for her, the smell of him against her, his chest smothering her, the stink of him.

I will kill him. I will kill him. And offer him. Will that please you, Apollo-Belinus? Esus? I can cut a piece for each of you. Cut him into pieces. Offer his scream. Make him scream. Grawnei, you did not scream. I did not hear you scream. Scream, Grawnei. Scream. Did I see two soldiers come from your room? No. Was it two? No. No. No.

FIFTEEN

Awake. But not. Somewhere there is a surface, and I must push through to true wakefulness. There. But no. Caught between worlds. That's it. Neither with the waking nor the sleeping. The living nor the dead.

Grawnei.

Neidriu.

I am coming. I will be there. I will be there.

Katha, are you there? Do you see me struggling? Katha. Can you help?

"Boudicca."

My name. Toward my name.

"Boudicca."

There is not enough air in this place. Katha. Katha. I will drown in this place of no water, no time. "Katha."

"I'm here." She squeezes my hand. That was the warmth I felt, the pressure. "There, breathe easy. Such a gasp you took. I feared it was your last breath."

"I couldn't wake up." The fire is high, the bed warm. My free hand travels the blanket tracing the thin form that is Neidriu. I gently slip my other hand from Katha's and run it along the other side of the blanket. Grawnei. Both of them curled toward me, now. In her sleep, Grawnei feels my touch and whimpers. "Shh, it's Mother. I'm here." She quiets. Katha's eyes are on me. Sorrowful eyes. Old eyes. She has grown old in the time that I slept. How long did I sleep? I have grown

79

old, too. Fatigued, even though I have just awakened. Katha. Will I be losing her soon? Is that death I see in her face–a hint, only a hint but there–a muddy moss shadow as if the earth has already started to claim her. I close my eyes against the thought.

"Will you sleep again?" she worries. "It was a deathly sleep. I didn't know if you'd return from it."

Yes, death wants me. I can feel it here, again, in the house, waiting, calling, so soon after it took Prasutagus. So insatiable, this death. Prasutagus, we need you now. Prasutagus. It takes some effort for me to speak. "How long did I sleep?"

"The night, the morning. It's midday."

"Did you rest?" I ask.

"I did, and Carduc watched over you while I slept."

The beating has wizened my flesh. It is taut in this shrunken state and will tear if I move. The bones, too, could not hide from the whip; they are brittle.

"Be still," Katha instructs, seeing me wince as I shift in the bed. "Don't move too much."

"Catus Decianus?" I whisper, reviling him that much more because I am forced to say his name.

"Don't think about him now. You have to heal."

"Katha, tell me."

"He's gone back to the village to round up more debtors. Flavinus was here earlier condemning Decianus's actions. He says Decianus acted without bidding by him, or Nero, or Paulinus."

"Then on whose bidding?"

"His own. He is looking to raise his position and thought this would put him in favor." She shakes her head. "Flavinus offered an apology."

"An apology?"

"He promises that you will not be disturbed again. You will not be forced from the house or from the land."

"Flavinus promises, and I'm to believe him because he promises?" My words are slow and labored. "Decianus will be back. If not him, someone else who seeks Nero's favor. Maybe Flavinus himself."

"Flavinus has been a friend," Katha protests. "He wouldn't hurt us."

"He has already hurt us by not restraining Decianus. We cannot stay here hoping for their goodwill, waiting for the next assault. We must go."

"Go where?" Katha asks, taking my hand again and sitting on the edge of the bed by Neidriu. "This is your home. Now rest. Just rest. Besides, little one," she adds sadly, "Rome is everywhere."

"There must be a spot in Britain where we could go and not be found," I argue. "In the north. We'll go as far north as we can. Past Brigante territory, up into..."

"Shh. Shh. Sit back, little one." She presses gently against my shoulder. "You can't go anywhere. Not now. Now you must rest and heal. And your daughters must heal. You're safe here."

"Until Decianus grows bored with his debtors and returns..."

"Shh."

"...and returns to abuse the bodies of my children." Neidriu's foot. Decianus's back. "Did you see what he did to her?"

"Shh. Don't cry. You'll wake her."

"I must protect her," I sob. "I must protect them. But how? If I flee, will Rome pursue us? Will they try to capture us and make us their slaves? Or perhaps they will send us to their arenas to be killed for sport. You know they do that in Rome, set fierce animals loose on their slaves and watch as they're torn to pieces. Is that the death I give my daughters if we flee now? Is that the punishment for trying to save them?"

"Shh," she interrupts, pushing me back again. "You must rest. You're not going to take your daughters anywhere. Now look. Shh," she whispers. "You're waking Neidriu."

"But if we stay...and what? Wait for Decianus to come back? How do I save my children, Katha?"

Neidriu nuzzles closer to me, hiding her face against my breast.

"Did I wake you, Neidriu? I'm sorry. But look, you're safe. You don't have to be afraid. And see, your sister is here on the other side of me. And there is Katha. We're all here and all safe. Let me see you. Let me see your face, Neidriu."

She shifts, and I think she will show me her face, but she moves her hands up to hide behind them.

"No, Neidriu. Don't hide from me. Why do you hide?" But I know why. Shame. "You have no reason to hide." This child now knows shame. That place on her little girl's body where all the commotion of life abounds has been made known to her now as a place of pain and defenselessness. A place of abuse, and now, for her, of loathing. How do I make her believe, now, that it is a place of love and of pleasure, a sacred place that links the worlds of the yet-born to the world of the born. A place of power. Neidriu. Not a place of shame.

"Here now." I lift her chin, and ease her hands away. As her eyes come up to meet mine, they brim with tears. Katha strokes her, as do I. Grawnei stirs. "Look, Neidriu, your sister is awake. Look, we're all here. Take her hand." I lift Grawnei's limp arm over my body and offer the hand to Neidriu. They hold each other for a short while, until Neidriu lets go, curls up to me again, and gives herself up to sleep.

But Grawnei is awake now, staring silently at the fire. Katha suggests a cup of milk. "Nice and sweet," she promises. "And one for your mother, too. You both need your strength."

Grawnei does not answer.

"And you, Katha," I say, "a cup for you, too."

She leaves the room, and I suffer with her absence, feeling suddenly unprotected. "Grawnei, how are you?" I try to bring safety back to the room with my voice. "The milk will be good, won't it?" She answers with silence, sorrowful silence. I yield to it and wait for Katha's return.

She brings the milk but can encourage Grawnei no better than I could. We allow the silence its reign and with our cups to our lips, each of us goes away from the other. Each of us goes to the remembering that this silence demands. Neidriu's foot. I reach for it and clasp it in my hand.

But, Grawnei. What does she remember? What is she seeing now? Two soldiers?

Two soldiers, Grawnei?

Katha wrestles free from her memory. "Rest," she tells me. "Sleep. Don't think of it. Pray, if you cannot stop the memories. You too, Grawnei. Say a prayer. Over and over. Apollo- Belinus, I honor you. Icena, I honor you. Let your prayers release your mind. Now lie back down, both of you."

Apollo-Belinus. Apollo-Belinus. Neidriu's foot. Two soldiers. Esus. Icena.

———

This time I awaken more readily, though a permanent sleep does seem to want to claim me. Katha, who has napped in the chair, opens her eyes when I do, as if we shared a dream. But I remember no dream.

"You should get up," she advises, rising stiffly. I see a bruise on her leg disappear under her tunic as she stands. "And walk a bit. If you don't, your wounds will knit too tightly. And you'll be like me, an old woman who can hardly raise herself from her chair. And the girls, let me give them a cedar tea to drink. It will run through them and wash them clean. Then I will bathe them and apply poultices."

"No," Neidriu protests, and though I cannot see under the cover, I can feel her move her hand between her legs.

"Shh. Are you awake?" I kiss her warm head.

"Just a cool poultice of the pulp of willow bark to relieve your pain," Katha assures Neidriu.

"It doesn't hurt," Neidriu insists, and then to me, she asks urgently, "Can't we stay in bed? I want to stay here."

"We can stay a while," I calm her. "I can tell you stories. Would you like that?"

"You really should get up," Katha frets. "And so should they."

"Shh. We will, soon. But first we'll have a story. All right, Neidriu? And Grawnei, are you awake?"

She does not answer.

"I know Grawnei likes stories, too. Don't you, Grawnei? She likes to listen to Carduc tell stories."

"Your mother used to like his stories, too, when she was a little one," Katha adds. "Oh yes. Carduc could tell her stories all day. And do you know what she would say at the end of the story? She would say 'Tell me another one.'"

I smile, remembering. "Yes, and do you know that I used to think? I used to think that Carduc was the son of a son of one of the giants who used to live here that he told me about."

Katha wrinkles her forehead with a question, and smiles.

"I did," I tell her. "When I was little." I turn to Neidriu, then to Grawnei–insistently silent–back and forth so they both have my attention. "He used to tell me about the giants who once lived here on the land, men and women the size of the tallest trees." Already my strength is waning. Like Neidriu, I would be satisfied to stay in bed all day, and all day tomorrow.

"Giants?" Neidriu asks in a voice that indicates she is willing herself to be interested. Cooperative child.

"Haven't I ever told you about the giants?"

She shakes her head.

"No?" It surprises me. Surely, I must have told her and she has forgotten. This was a story told to me as a child, one of the first stories I knew of Britain. I must have told her. "Grawnei, have I told you? You know about the giants, don't you?" Surely if I didn't tell her, Carduc did.

No answer.

"Tell about them," Neidriu persuades me, arranging herself on her side so that she can see me.

"Well, these giants had such strength that if a mountain were in their way, they would simply lift it and move it. No one would ever come to Britain because of fear of the giants. But everyone in the world had heard how beautiful this land was, how clear the rivers ran, how green the hills were. And so one day, two brave men, Brutus and Corineus, set out from Troy to come to the land of the giants."

Yes, this is a good story to tell. It is assuring me with a sense of continuation, a reminder that there was a time before yesterday, and there will be a time after. Our lives are greater than yesterday's events.

"Now, the giants were not a peaceful people. They often fought among themselves. 'This is my territory,' one giant would say. 'No, it's mine,' another would argue, and so they'd battle over it. And when one or the other of them fell, the whole island would shake, and the ground there would cave in. That's how we've come to have our valleys." I remember the story well and remember, as a child, trying to fix a face on the giant.

"The strongest of the giants was an ugly one named Gogmagog, and by the time Corineus and Brutus arrived here, Gogmagog had killed most of the other giants. Now, he wanted to rid the island of Corineus and Brutus. But Gogmagog, like the other giants, had one weakness, and it didn't take Brutus and Corineus long to figure it out. Do you want to know what that weakness was?" I ask.

Neidriu shakes her head. Grawnei expresses no curiosity.

"Well, once a giant fell," I continue, "he could not get back up. So, Corineus and Brutus set out to topple Gogmagog. But no matter how hard they pushed, they couldn't knock him over. No matter how they tried to trip him, they couldn't make him fall. At first, Gogmagog enjoyed the game that he thought the two men from Troy were playing with him. But then he grew tired of it and told Corineus and Brutus that he'd fling them from his land back into the sea where they had come from. Now Corineus and Brutus had to make sure Gogmagog didn't catch them. It was not difficult to hide from him as giants can see far but they can't see near. As long as Corineus and Brutus stayed close to him, Gogmagog couldn't see them. This gave them the chance to observe Gogmagog. They discovered that despite the fact that he never slept, he never seemed to tire. Corineus and Brutus began to believe they'd have to give up. But then one day, Brutus noticed something."

"What?" Neidriu asks, giving herself and her pain over to this tale.

"He and Corineus were exhausted from chasing and being chased so they were resting and hiding on Gogmagog's feet, holding on around his ankles which were as wide as tree trunks. Gogmagog couldn't see them, of course, so he kept running through the woods searching for them. When he came to a mountain, instead of moving it, Gogmagog leaped over it. While they were up in the air, Brutus noticed that the strength seemed to go out of Gogmagog's legs. His muscles became slack. But as soon as he landed, the muscles tightened again. Brutus realized that in some way the giant took his strength from the land, and if his feet were not firmly planted on the ground, if he was not connected to the land, he became weak.

"So, Corineus and Brutus devised a plan to get Gogmagog's feet off the ground. They jumped off the giant's feet, and Corineus ran ahead, waving to Gogmagog so he would chase him. Brutus followed behind, closely watching Gogmagog's feet. Corineus ran and ran, finally scrambling up and over the hill that had figured into their plan. To Gogmagog, the hill was nothing more than a bump in the land, and in his desire to catch Corineus he leaped easily over it. For just a moment, both his feet were off the ground, and that was when Brutus struck. He hurled a rock no bigger than my fist at Gogmagog and sent him crashing to the ground.

"They killed him?" Neidriu asks.

"Yes, and once the other giants heard of Gogmagog's death, they fled from the island, afraid of the two men from Troy. Now the land belonged to Corineus and Brutus, and since Brutus was the one who killed Gogmagog, they named the land Britain after Brutus, and Cornwall in the west where Gogmagog was killed was named for Corineus."

Grawnei's body slackens a bit; her attention releases itself from me. But Neidriu is not satisfied. "But it was Gogmagog's land first," she says. "Why did they have to kill him?" I smile at her question, at the simple fairness which she wants to apply.

"Gogmagog would have killed them if they didn't kill him."

"But they should have left him alone. He didn't do anything wrong." She is near tears again.

"No." I hug her. "He didn't do anything wrong." And a bitter realization occurs to me. This story is being enacted again, but now we are the giants and Rome is Corineus and Brutus, and the land was ours first. It is a fine story for those who are not the giants. But what of those who are the giants? And Neidriu, with her child's wisdom and her sensitive heart, knows that she should abhor the story. Instead of the warriors I have always thought of them as, Corineus and Brutus now seem greedy and impetuous, crude in their disregard for Gogmagog's life. Like Rome in their disregard for us.

"They didn't have to kill him," Neidriu decides.

"Ah, but he is not really killed," Katha comes to my aid. "He is in a long sleep. There are rises in the west where Gogmagog fell, and they say that if you look from a distance, you can see him resting peacefully." She moves her hand to indicate a mound, "His feet here," her hand goes flat then rises again, "knees there, big belly," she makes an exaggerated movement, "chin, nose and brow. And someday, he will wake up again."

"Oh." Neidriu is willing to accept this, but wonders, "Will he be angry?"

"No," Katha assures her, "he will be friendly."

Neidriu allows herself to be satisfied. But I am not so willing to accept. He will be angry; he should be angry, and if he were those rises in the west, he would awaken and destroy us. How many other of our stories tell of glory at the expense of an entire people? Rome will speak of their glory, too, here on Britain where they raped children and beat women. They will tell their sons and daughters and will drink a cup of wine as they tell, and their children, except for the rare simple-hearted one like Neidriu, will clap their hands at the tale and ask for more.

"Grawnei, are you still awake? How do you feel?"

She won't answer, and it is as though she is traveling away from me, riding away, wanting me to catch her. But I can't. "Grawnei." I know why she chooses silence; with silence she can remove herself from this place. It is a way of not being here, of not existing, and if she doesn't exist, nothing more can happen to her. I remember. I remember wanting silence when Tallas was killed. I remember thinking there would be solace there. But there is no solace. And there is no true silence.

"Tell me another story," Neidriu requests sleepily. "A story about my father." Prasutagus is dead. A day ago I thought his death would be the hardest thing my daughters would ever have to bear. "He was a good father. I don't think there was ever a king who loved his daughters more." That is true. And he could not have known Decianus would come. He could not have. Yet, he was a friend to Rome. All along, he worried first about pleasing Rome. "You know that sometimes when a baby is born to a king and a queen, the baby is sent away from the house to be raised by someone else. It is called fosterage," I tell Neidriu, struggling to disbelieve what Decianus wants me to believe of Prasutagus. Prasutagus, did you know? "Then when the baby has grown and become an adult, she is brought back to the king's house. When I was born, my father did not send me away. Instead, he brought someone in to raise me: Katha. She had just lost her own baby during the birth, and it was her milk I drank. My father loved me too much to send me away. When I was older, he would sometimes come to me at night and tell me stories."

"But my father," Neidriu interrupts, "tell me about my father."

Your father left us here at the mercy of Rome. Your father died when he was most needed. Your father made an arrangement for our futures that has been our doom. Prasutagus, what have you done to us? "Your father could never have sent you away."

But perhaps it would have been better if he had. Then you would not have been here when Decianus came. Then it would only have been me here, and I could bear that.

"Are you in pain?" Katha asks.

My anguish must show on my face. "I must be tired. My thoughts are wandering." I pause again, then continue, "Neidriu, do you remember how your father used to hoist you onto his horse and take you riding with him? You too, Grawnei. And Neidriu, you used to crawl on your hands and knees into the room where he and the council met. You crept right under the table and sat at his feet. How many kings would allow their daughters to attend such council meetings? Only one, I think. And he watched you, Grawnei, did you know that? When you weren't looking, he would watch you." I would not embarrass her by telling her that I had seen her watching him, too. It seems that that would be a secret she would not want discovered. "He watched you play; he watched you work; he watched you sleep. He loved having his eyes on you, seeing you learn and grow, watching your forehead furrow as you figured a solution to a problem. He thought you were very clever. And you are."

"And me?" Neidriu inquires, hopefully.

"And you. He watched you, too."

Katha suggests soup, and I realize that I am hungry. When she leaves, Grawnei's silence casts a pall over the three of us. "I have a secret," I whisper impulsively, growing unreasonably uneasy with her silence, needing to dispel it in some way.

"About our father?" Neidriu asks.

"About all of us. Your father, my father, me, all of us. Do you know that at one time we carried swords?" Our carrying swords is just a story now, a thing of the past, like Gogmagog, but they need to hear stories of our strength now. I need to tell stories of our strength. "By now you both would have had swords of your own, light swords, and you would have been good with them, I'm sure. Do you want to see something? Something no one else has seen? A secret? Do you? Grawnei?"

She will not answer, but her eyes are on me. Neidriu nods.

"Get up."

We rise slowly, each of us protecting our sorest spots.

"It hurts," Neidriu whines, pressing her hand between her legs. Grawnei touches herself there, too, but in embarrassment, quickly takes her hand away. Neidriu needs to pass water, and I give her the shallow cauldron and have her squat over it. Whimpers accompany her stream. The sting. I can almost feel it myself. My face and Grawnei's reflect Neidriu's grimace.

When she is back in bed, she whispers, "Come."

"Soon, but do you see me? I am here, and I see you. Rest. I will not leave the room."

"And Grawnei."

"Grawnei, too. She is here."

When Neidriu is reassured, I kneel–feeling welts open on my legs, and on my back–roll away the mat away, and begin digging. But soon the position is too painful, and I stand again. "Dig there," I instruct Grawnei, hoping the sword is still there–it has been so long since I looked for it.

She does, and when her fingers come to something, she casts a dull look at me.

"Keep going." I point with my foot to show the length of the opening in the earth she needs to make. She continues. "Careful," I warn when she has dug out the area and is reaching in. "Gently."

She leans forward on her knees and lifts the bundle. I bend to take it from her, and she comes to her feet slowly, not with the scramble of a young girl but with the ache of an old woman. When I unsheathe the sword, she opens her mouth as though to gasp but no sound comes out. "Touch the blade," I tell her. "It will be cool." She lays a thin finger on the flat of the metal, then traces with that finger the vine of engravings that runs its length. The blade is clean. There is no degradation. Carduc. Somehow, he has tended it. In the night. Or while we were out. I do not know when. But its gleam assures me that he has been attentive to it while I was not. "That's the hilt, and the pommel." She touches the smooth enamel embeddings. "Take it like this." With my arms encircling her from behind, I clasp my hands around hers and steady them. "This was my father's sword, your grandfather's. It was to be mine. Someday, yours. Is it heavy?" I ease my grip a bit, forcing her to take up the bulk of the weight. The blade dips. She grunts at the strain, and I am happy for another sound.

Her shoulders soon tremble with the effort, and a quiver skips up each arm. I take the weight again. "Having the sword in my hands made me feel brave. Does it make you feel brave?"

I do not know how long Carduc has been standing at the entry to the room, but when I look up, he is there.

"Now we must put it away," I tell Grawnei. "And you are not to dig it up without me. No one can ever know it is here. No one." It was reckless of me to show her the sword; I realize that now that the deed has been witnessed. Anyone could have seen. But if it must be someone, best that it is Carduc. Grawnei helps me bury it; she smoothes the dirt and pulls the mat back to its place. Then she sits there. Keeper of the sword.

Carduc is gone. I shuffle out to the hearth where Katha is preparing bowls of soup. "Carduc was just here," I say.

"He's gone to the work hut," she answers. "He'll be back."

Neidriu cries out, and I hurry back to the room.

"You were gone," she accuses me.

"I'm not gone. I'm here. I'm right here. I thought you were sleeping."

"Don't leave me."

"I won't leave you. But look, your sister is here. You weren't alone. Grawnei, come and take your sister's hand. Katha has prepared soup. We will eat. We will heal. My daughters are strong. Neidriu, can you be strong?" Her eyes are teary, but she nods that she can be. "Grawnei?" She will not nod; that would be too much like a spoken answer. "Neidriu, you will have to help your sister be strong. Can you help her?" She nods again, tentatively, and casts a quick frightened look at Grawnei.

Katha, always with an instinct to calm, tells the girls about a litter that a herder's bitch has dropped this morning. "Perhaps we can go to see them," she suggests, smiling. "Perhaps, even, the girls would like a pup. What do you think your mother would say to a pup?"

My tears surprise me. I am able to stifle them, but Katha sees, and quickly takes me into the haven of her arms. "What is it?"

It is the thought of pups; it is Katha's way of chasing worry away–of having a cake, a drink, a pup ready for the offering. "I love you," I tell her, and tears come to her eyes, too. Neidriu, frightened by our emotion, kneels on the bed and reaches for us. Katha and I move closer, letting Neidriu wrap her arms around us. "Come, Grawnei." She kneels, too, and reaches to us, and though her presence is a weak one–she will not put up her arms to complete our circle- -she is with us. Together, that way, we ask for the gods' protection.

Katha breaks the circle to bring us the soup, and as we sip on it in our bed, she sends for Leanan, and I realize by the way her head pulls back just slightly that my appearance is alarming. She inquires about my condition and the condition of my daughters, but she looks beyond me as she asks, a gesture not of rudeness but of modesty and respect. To look into my face would be to see there what happened, and she wants me to know that she is refusing to see my daughters and me in that disgrace. "We are well," I tell her. "Let everyone know that we are well."

She nods. "They will be relieved."

"Katha says that one of the herder's bitches has dropped her litter. My daughters would like a pup. Would you choose one for them?" She is glad to have a task to do for me, and agrees that a pup will cheer the girls.

I see a quick dagger. A dagger penetrating Decianus's flesh. With Neidriu and Grawnei so in need of me, I can only let my thoughts wander away from them for a moment; I can only briefly indulge my vengeance. But I can see his face as the pain twists it. I can see myself yanking the dagger from him, and burying it again to the hilt.

But then Prasutagus warns as if he is still here, "Do nothing, Boudicca. Bear it. You cannot stand against Rome. Do nothing. Forget. Try to forget. It is the only way to survive."

Katha urges me to finish my soup. She, too, would like me to forget, would like to keep me from thinking about it.

We sleep on and off, and day passes into evening. Katha bathes my skin with her boiled poplar buds and beeswax that she has used on my cuts and bruises since I was a child, and for a short while afterward, I have relief from the stinging and can move more freely.

We sleep again, and in the morning Leanan brings two pups so newly born that they haven't yet opened their eyes. The way she cradles them reminds me of her two sons, still slaves in Camulodumnum; Decianus clearly has no intention of sending for them. I had almost forgotten about her suffering. This is what Rome does—renders suffering so great that it allows one to forget that others suffer, also. Where once we were a tribe, now we are singular, each enduring her own agony.

The pups' scrawny bodies twitch with cold. "They must be returned to their mother," Leanan explains, "to nurse. But in six weeks time, when they can see and have found their legs, and their mother's milk dries up, I will bring them back to you."

Neidriu smiles and points to the pup in the crux of Leanan's left arm. "I want that one, the one with the stripe on his ear."

"Good," Leanan coos, scratching the ear. "We'll remember him by his stripe. And look, Grawnei, do you see the paw on this one, how it is a lighter color than the others? That's how we'll remember yours."

Grawnei puts a finger to the paw.

Leanan smiles at me before she leaves. Once we were young girls, dreaming of husbands and children.

The pups are not the only gifts the girls receive that day. Later, after Katha has bathed me again in the oil, Carduc reappears. He presents each of the girls with a dagger and a leather belt. "For hunting," he says, looking at me for approval. "They are old enough to hunt, both of them. I will teach them. First, they will learn to throw. Maybe they will bring home a field mouse. They should keep their daggers at their sides. That is the Iceni way."

I do not object. Grawnei gets up to strap the belt to her waist, but I must unstrap it when she lies back down in bed. If nothing else, it will give them an activity. Carduc is a good teacher. Let him tell them stories of warriors such as Vercingetorix. Let him show them how to kill with daggers. And if these lessons will teach Grawnei to speak again, then let her learn.

Later that day, we spend some time out of bed, though by afternoon we are back in its safety, Neidriu pushing up against me, Grawnei, close, quiet. It is forgetful sleep that they crave most now, forgetful and protective, and they slip greedily toward it.

Katha will not go to her own bed despite my insistence.

"The house is well guarded," I remind her; she holds her tongue but I know by her turned down mouth what remark she would make if she weren't worried about upsetting me. And what good did our guards do when we needed them? It's true; unarmed, they are impotent. But the illusion of their protection will have to serve for now.

"I'll sleep here," she answers, indicating the chair she has spent the last two nights in.

"No. You need rest. Take Grawnei's bed if you insist on being in the house."

I can see in the way her face goes soft and her eyes, heavy, that she happily anticipates a bed. "If you think you'll be all right," she agrees.

"Good night."

"I'll be nearby," she assures me.

But when she has left us and the girls are asleep, I miss her companionship and can't quiet my mind. Decianus. Neidriu's foot. Grawnei in her room with two soldiers. Prasutagus, did you know? Decianus's back. The whip.

What was that noise? Decianus? Where is Katha? Killed? And the guards? Killed? No. Nothing.

My legs are restless, as if they want to carry me away from my thoughts, and the motion is disturbing the girls and exacerbating my pain. I am suffering this way when Carduc calls quietly into the room and asks for permission to enter. I happily grant it, assuming that Katha could not comfortably leave us unattended, and so assigned Carduc to keep watch tonight. I am hoping he has mixed a tea that will soothe me.

"How are your wounds?" he asks.

"They'll heal. The oils help."

"And the children?"

I look to each of them. "Neidriu is afraid. Grawnei won't speak."

"Grawnei was always a quiet child," he remarks.

"And Neidriu a nervous one," I add. "I'm glad when they can sleep. And forget."

"It's tempting to forget. To let the wounds heal and forget. To sleep and forget."

"Yes."

"That is what Prasutagus would want–for you to forget," he says. "And that is what Rome would want." He seems to challenge me.

"To forget? Do you think I could forget that my daughters were raped?"

He doesn't answer, and I hear his silence as an accusation, and all my anguish erupts. "Is that what you think of me, Carduc, that all I want is to forget what happened? That I am capable of forgetting? Of pretending that I didn't see what Decianus did to Neidriu? Do you think I will ever stop seeing that, or ever stop wanting to kill him?"

Again, he doesn't respond, and I continue, glad to say to him what has been on my mind for a long time. "Ever since I stopped practicing with the sword, you've shown disdain for me, and disappointment. Why? Because I didn't want to deceive Prasutagus anymore? Because I accepted my role as his wife? It was you who told me to accept the role, Carduc. You, who told me to go to my marriage with dignity–a marriage Rome wanted. So, I went with dignity, and yes, I found some happiness in the marriage, and for that you have accused me."

He waits to see if I will have more to say, but my anger is only frustrating me. When he sees that I will not continue, he answers, "I don't accuse you. You accuse yourself."

"How do I accuse myself, Carduc?"

"I was not disappointed in you. But I believe you were disappointed in yourself."

"And why was I disappointed in myself?" I ask impatiently.

"Because you loved Prasutagus. You believed I thought you were weak because of that love, but it's you who thinks yourself weak."

"Oh, but you think I'd try to forget what happened to my daughters. Isn't that weakness?"

"What happened, happened to you as well."

"And I would kill Catus Decianus for it if I could," I assert venomously.

Now he looks at me as though he intends to see through me, intends to find something in my eyes, my face.

I hold his gaze and let him look.

"I see that you would," he whispers.

SIXTEEN

Two days pass in a confusion of sleep, anger, anxiety. Neidriu cries frequently; the tumult of her emotions is frightening to her, and she is harder and harder to calm. Her praying is continuous. I believe she is afraid that if she stops, Decianus will come again. The days since the ordeal bring us no farther from it; it is with us, settling deeper, permanently into our bodies. Grawnei is no closer to speaking. And me, each sound alerts me to the possibility of Decianus's return. Flavinus's repeated assurances grant me no peace, and I grow more and more fretful as I try to imagine what the next day will bring, the next weeks. Over and over, I attempt to see our future. But it is as if there will be none; my mind can only conceive of the recent violent past, and an ongoing present in which we live as we do now, fearfully, watchfully.

What I hear of the village is that no one is about. Word of Decianius's deeds has spread and people are keeping themselves unseen as though their invisibility might protect them from him, might allow him to forget their existence. To stay alive we must appear to have ceased to exist.

Leanan has persuaded the girls to visit the pups, and reluctant as they are to leave me, they cannot resist, and I am grateful to Leanan for her effort to restore some of their independence.

Carduc comes regularly now and inquires about my recovery. Thanks to the salves, my welts have cooled and my skin grows more pliant. He treats me differently since he came into my room the other night; he is no longer as aloof. And though I am still distrusting of him,

I must admit, there is a vague sense of opportunity that I get when he comes to see me, as if I could say something to him or he to me that would set everything right, as if there is safety somewhere in our old friendship.

He comes again while the girls are visiting the pups and I am resting in bed. Like my daughters, I find protection there. I show Carduc my arms so he can see the hint of healing. He examines them, and his eyes rest on the old scar, a thin white line cutting across my forearm.

"You were full of rebellion, then," he says.

I trace the scar with my finger. "Yes." I remember the day I cut myself, remember my desperation. "It reminds me of Tallas," I admit. He waits quietly while my mind wanders back. "Do you know Grawnei is his?" I ask, not sure why I want to offer him this confidence, but suspicious that he already knows. "He would have loved her if he could, and he would not accept this treatment of his daughter."

"Nor of you," Carduc adds. Is there a suggestion in his voice, instigation?

"And I should not accept it, either. Is that what you are here to tell me?" I ask quietly. "But what can I do? How do I respond without risking more abuse? Rome can do what it wants with me. But Neidriu and Grawnei, Carduc. If I retaliate what do you think will become of them?" I shake my head to dispel the images that form quickly. "And yet, you're right, how do I do nothing? These are the king's daughters, the queen's daughters." I clasp my hands in despair, and I want Carduc to nod, to take one of my hands, to show me that he sees the intolerably unsolvable nature of the situation, to counsel forbearance.

Instead he says, "You showed Grawnei your father's sword. Why?"

"I hoped it would distract her a little, give her courage. I told her it gave me courage."

"Does it?"

"I don't know. It used to. It reminds me of strength whether that strength is mine or not."

"Are you well enough to walk?" he asks.

"I think so," I answer, perplexed, having expected him to have asked if I was ready to start practicing with the sword again.

"To my work hut?" he continues.

"In the hills? That is a good distance. Why?"

"There is something there that you should see."

"Carduc...the soldiers, Decianus's men..." I stammer, my fear showing, my confusion, and my impatience for him returning. Why would he ask something of me that he knows I am not well enough to do? It is the same sense I felt from him the other night–a challenge. Why does he challenge me? "You have permission to be in the woods. But I would be stopped," I remind him. "If Decianus..."

"You would come at night. No one would see you. There are few soldiers patrolling the woods. And the ones who do are lazy and too afraid to enter too deeply. Paulinus's attack on Mona is still fresh in their imaginations, and they fear that the Druids' spirits wander the woods. And there is dissension among them, also. Some favored Paulinus's attack. Others objected. Some will favor the attack on you; others will worry over it. They argue among themselves and give more attention to these arguments than to their patrolling duties. And they keep their wine sacks as close companions."

"I can't leave my daughters," I argue. "Neither of them sleeps through the night. If they awaken and I'm not here..."

"They will not awaken. I will see to that."

"How? A sleeping potion?"

"A mild one in their milk. It will not harm them, and in the morning they will feel better for having slept so restfully. It will be a healing sleep."

"Carduc..." I do not want to go. I am afraid. He knows I am afraid. Does he want me to say it aloud? I am afraid. Is this another one of his lessons in which I am to discover that which I already know? Then I already know that I am afraid. "What do you have there at your hut? Tell me. I don't think I'm ready for such a long walk."

"You must see it," he insists.

Why this challenge when I thought he was trusting me again, when I was prepared to begin trusting him? I am afraid. He knows I am afraid. Why does he taunt me? Why does he demand more than I am capable of? A trick, to get me out of bed? To prove that I have courage? But I have no courage. He looks steadily at me. When I do not answer, he drops his eyes to my arm, the old scar, invokes Tallas with this glance, then looks back at me.

I surrender to him, but it is not out of courage or strength. He is wrong if he thinks it is. It is out of weakness. I am too weak to admit my fear to him, too weak to argue. "I'll come."

———

So, I am to go into the night woods. What will be there? What must I see? A Druid? Has Carduc found a surviving Druid, one who has been wandering the woods? Will there be a sacrifice? Human? But the Iceni do not practice that. Are we to begin? Catus Decianus? Will he have been captured? Will Carduc expect me to kill him?

When the girls return, they are not as heavy-hearted as when they left. To keep their minds on the pleasure the pups they have visited give them, I suggest they each begin weaving a mat. "When you go back to your own beds, as soon you will have to do, your pups can lie alongside on their mats."

Neidriu frowns at the prospect of going back to her own bed but is excited about the project. Grawnei expresses nothing but is not resistant. Leanan stays to assist them.

I can think again of what awaits me in the woods, and I am angry, once more, at Carduc for his insistence, his secrecy, and yet I must admit some excitement, a quick change in me. This trip into the woods, reckless as it may be, has given me something to anticipate other than Decianus's return. There is a hopefulness in the prospect of my being up, moving, a sense that the days in bed, in fear, in expectation of the worst can end. I will get up. I will resume a life, the way I resumed life once before. Clever Carduc. Perhaps that is all he has in mind with this trip to the woods–a desire to persuade me from my bed, to move me from this place of lifelessness, hopelessness, to a spot in the woods where he will me show me how my life can be mine again.

In the evening, Katha brings the girls sweet milk, and I see to it that they drink all of it. Carduc is right; they sleep soundly and their limbs twitch as the strain of these last days releases them. Their slack weight sinks into the bed. When I am satisfied that they will not awaken, I get up and dress, strap my dagger to my waist and wait for Carduc. In the quiet night, though, my mind can't imagine the hopefulness I conceived of earlier. It can only conjure Decianus, again and again. And I am leaving my children alone. If they wake...If they are awakened...If Decianus comes...

I shake Katha from Grawnei's bed. "Carduc is taking me into the woods. If I do not return, you are to raise my daughters as your own. Keep them from Roman hands. Swear that you will."

She swears and mumbles herself into wakefulness. "What's he got you up to?" she asks and shuffles out to the hearth where she prepares a small sack of honey cakes for me.

"I don't know, Katha."

———

With little more than a look and a nod from him, I am following Carduc on foot across our fields, using an indirect route to the woods, avoiding the village and the Roman fort. At the boundary of my property we climb over the dry mud wall at a spot where it is crumbling–I remind myself to have it repaired; the time of not needing walls is over–and make our way west. The welts on my legs and across my back, which seemed to be healing, prickle again, hot and taut.

Once in the woods, out of the open, I expect to feel protected, but the sudden cooing of an owl startles me, and I dart away from the sound and feel another welt open on my thigh. All around are noises, and I must consciously identify each one or be startled breathless by it. That is the distant stream running unimpeded by ice, not a Roman soldier tramping. The rustle near the ground is chipmunks, mice. The exhalation, there it is again, is the wind. That clean snapping of twigs is a doe as she leaps and lands.

We wend deeper into the woods, guiding ourselves trunk to trunk. There is no path and the newly waxing moon only lights the distance of a stride or two; my eyes are slow to adjust, and I must feel for the ground with each step, not knowing whether the land might slope away from me. Then for a moment, there is a sense of familiarity–I did run in these woods as a young girl–and an old confidence is roused. But where I expect to find something (this is where the tree with two trunks will be), it is not there, and quickly, the confidence is forgotten. I stumble over fallen branches and ruptured earth which spits thick roots, and a disquiet churns in me so that I can taste it rising in my throat, and I know the scent of it is on me, and every creature nearby sniffs it in the air. Carduc travels as though he is alone–quickly, determinedly, without a word.

Happily, it is not long before we come to the jutting rocks, and now, finally, surely, I know this spot and know that just over the rise I will see my tree of worship and will know where I am. Its height will rise there. There. But where is it? Here are the sister trees which stand thin-trunked, side to side, but my tree which should be here. "Carduc." Now I see. Struck by lightning, the upper half of the trunk has collapsed and makes a bridge in the air where it caught on the trunk of a tree to its south.

Carduc sees. "Come," he urges.

With hands unsteadied by cold, exertion, fear, I fumble with the sack tied at my waist and toss a handful of crumbled cake toward the tree, but cannot think of a words to make a prayer.

"Come," Carduc repeats.

I am glad to go; the collapsed tree warns me away.

The sound of the travelling water becomes louder, and we follow it to the stream, and hurry along the bank against the water's flow. At a place where the stream widens, Carduc's hut comes into view. I approach slowly, fatigued and worried about what I will find. Has he saved another item of my father's? My guesses begin again. Who will greet me here? What will be expected of me? Before we continue, Carduc bends to the stream, fills a sack and offers me water. I drink thirstily.

We do not enter his workplace, but at a spot where the earth is scattered with patchy moss and small stones, a spot no different from any other, unmarked in any obvious way, Carduc kneels and begins to dig. At once I understand that my father's was not the only sword buried and that Carduc has managed to hide his, too. But what are two swords? Why did he think it necessary for me to see his? I kneel, too, slowly, stiffly, an old woman kneeling, and begin to dig. The earth is cool, and Carduc has buried his secret deeply. At last, my fingers scrape at something hard; Carduc digs faster, then brushes the dirt away, and I see, not a sword, but a chest of iron. He gouges out the earth around the chest until he is able to slide his hand in and lift the lid.

In this grave, under a cloth, lie at least two dozen sheathed swords. He lets me gaze at them, watches me put my hand into the ground and feel the leather scabbards, the cold metal of their exposed hilts.

"There are other such spots," he says, after my hands have satisfied themselves.

"How?" I look for an explanation.

"Rome has no interest in what I do up here."

"You've been forging swords?" I try to understand.

"Mine are not the only ones," he tells me. "When your father learned we would be disarmed, he sent me out to spread the word to those whom he believed he could trust, those who would never betray the tribe to Rome. 'Yield one sword to Rome, bury another,' he instructed. 'Do nothing to make Rome suspicious. If you own only one sword, surrender it; but if you have more than one, and you can trust yourself not to use it until the time is right, then bury one.' The Roman soldiers have no fondness for our long swords," Carduc continues.

I shake my head to show confusion.

"They find them unwieldy, and prefer their own short swords. The swords they took at the disarming are still somewhere in the territory, at the fort, perhaps. I never saw them carted out; they would not risk crossing from here to the west with wagons full of swords. And the fort here is not equipped for melting weapons down. Their weapons-makers and their large kilns are in the west and in the south." He begins to speak more quickly. "Paulinus is in the west, as you know, with the concentration of the army with him. But soon he will move east. We will not be so unguarded again."

I continue to shake my head, even as an understanding begins to come to me.

"Think of Neidriu," he urges. "And Grawnei. See what was done to them. See it. Think of Tallas. See him and what was done to him. Can you be unsure?"

Something takes his attention away from me before I can answer, and he inclines his head to one side where he listens for a sound, which I cannot hear. His eyes move slowly across the night, then settle in the direction of the stream. He gestures for me to go to the hut, but I do not obey. I draw my dagger and look for what he sees, but he grabs the dagger from me, and with a quick looping of the rope at his waist, secures it to his body. Silently, he closes the chest, covers it with dirt. We stay crouched as a figure comes into view, a Roman patroller. He enters the hut, and Carduc pulls me up. "Go," he whispers, but a voice stops me.

"Who is there?" the soldier shouts, unsheathing his short sword.

Carduc does not hesitate. "Carduc, the iron worker. That is my hut there. I have permission from Flavinus to work here."

"Your permission is rescinded," the Roman announces, coming closer. "No one is to be in the hills. And what is it that brings you here in the middle of the night?"

"I often work at night," Carduc explains.

"I see what your work is," the Roman says, espying me, but not yet recognizing me. "Let's go," he says, still pointing his sword our way. "We'll see what Flavinus says of your midnight meeting." Slung on a strap over his shoulder is a trumpet that he reaches for to alert the rest of the patrol from which he must have become separated.

When the soldier lets his sword dip, Carduc lurches forward, knocks him to the ground, picks up a small rock and strikes him three, four, five times on the head. At last, the body goes limp. "Quickly," Carduc directs me, lifting the man under his arms. "His legs." Awkwardly and without a secure hold, I take the patroller by his boots. But I am too weak to carry him and drop the heavy legs to the ground. Carduc drags him, stumbling down the bank; I follow to the water, and wade behind him into the stream. The shock of the icy water revives the Roman; he gasps, coughs, spits and struggles to stand. Carduc pushes at his head and his shoulders, submerging him once more. The Roman thrashes; I move alongside him, grab a boot but cannot hold it with all the kicking he does. Still, I prevent him from finding his balance. His arms beat the surface, and he grasps frantically for something and finds the edge of my cloak. He tugs; I pull back but cannot release his grasp, and so must move closer to relieve the tension that his yanking is causing at my neck where the cloak is tied and clasped. Heavier and heavier, the water is dragging on me. The Roman and the water. Minerva protect me.

"Hold him," Carduc hisses.

Still, the Roman has my cloak. Let me go. Let me go. Under my feet, the bed of the stream shifts, but I hold myself in a steady squat, push down on the Roman chest, down on his shoulder. He resists wildly, breaks the surface with his head, gasps, gurgles. My hand finds his throat, slippery and wet and twisting like a fish, but I squeeze and push at once. Carduc's hand goes over mine, tightening my grip, forcing the Roman neck downward, downward. Squeezing until I feel flesh and muscle yield, collapse.

The tugging at my cloak eases. The thrashing ceases. Still we hold him. Carduc's hands over mine. Longer. Longer.

Longer.

Tentatively, Carduc releases his hold; his hands hover over mine, ready to apply them again if the Roman begins a fresh resistance. But he is still.

"Let him go."

I bring my hands out of the water. The weight of the boots, the helmet, the leather of his uniform keep the Roman from bobbing to the surface; but he does not sink either, not yet, rather floats, suspended below the surface.

With a shove, Carduc sends the body into the current. Before I turn back, I silently offer this Roman to Minerva. Carduc and I help each other to the bank.

Still breathing heavily, he reproaches me, "You must be careful. A dagger wound on a Roman would have brought an inquiry. A drowning in the river will be considered a careless accident. We cannot draw their attention now. Come, we must return. The patrollers may be looking for this man."

I cannot answer.

I dart behind him now, silently, adroitly. Fear carries me, but it is not only fear. Exultation? I only know that we are home quickly, and I am at my hearth, drying, and my blood will not stop pounding.

SEVENTEEN

His face floats toward me. I push on it, but it does not stay submerged. Rising, closer and closer, I push again but have no strength. Stay down. He won't stay down. Stay down. He fights so fiercely, this man with his instinct to preserve himself. Just a man. A frightened man. Now I have killed a man, a frightened man, and this trembling will not cease. My feet will not warm. I have killed a man, and I see now what I am capable of. I can kill.

I can kill.

His face rises again. Is he one of the soldiers who left Grawnei's room? Is he one of the two? Then I could kill him again. Yes, each time his face rises, I will kill him. Every Roman is one of the two. A frightened man, and wasn't Grawnei frightened?

I can kill.

I have killed. Tomorrow will not be the same as today. No day from here on will be the same as the days before this. Because now I have killed a man. A Roman man.

Prasutagus, are you glad you are dead? Glad you did not live to see me perform this deed? But you left me to do it. Do you see what you left me to do?

They will come for me. I am afraid. Afraid. I have always been afraid. I see that now. But no, not always. Since Tallas's death. Since your death, Tallas. But no, before that. Since your capture. Even before that. Since the day the messenger came to my father's house and told us of your rebellion. I have been afraid since then. All these years. Even when I thought I was happy, there was fear beneath the happiness, always fear for what I knew they were capable of. Pacify them, I thought. Hide from them. Live quietly, and they will leave me alone. See how they left me alone? You raised bees, Tallas. I remember your bees, and you would not have forgotten that a bee's nature is to sting. I tried to make myself believe that if I did what they asked, I could live with them in their hive. Their hive that was once our land. But all the while, in some place in me, there was fear, fear for what I knew their true nature to be.

But now see me? I have killed a man. And what is my true nature?

There will be more killing.

No.

But there will be. I see that. The swords. My sword. It is no mere talisman, left to me by my father to remind me of strength and hope. It is a weapon. He left me a weapon.

There will be killing.

And that face, the Roman face, it floats toward me, and I must kill him, again.

EIGHTEEN

I do not sleep.

The face floats up.

By morning, I am sure that suspicion will have been aroused; the body will have been found, and it will be revealed that I did the killing. How do I act? The way I sit, stand, turn my head announce my guilt. I killed a man. I wear it on every part of my body.

Grawnei and Neidriu still sleep heavily. I join Katha and Carduc at the hearth, watching Carduc to see how I should behave, waiting to let him instruct me–if he drinks, I will drink. If he eats, I will eat. He says nothing; I do not speak. Katha must know, surely Carduc has told her, and if not, she must see it on me, smell it on me. But do I speak of it? No. Act as though it did not happen? Yes, that is the safest way. Why, then, does he look at me that way, as if he expects something? What? My body is so sore. Even my jaw, as I chew the bread, aches. Why does he look so inquiringly at me, so expectantly? He wants something. What? Is it about the swords? I cannot pretend I didn't see them, cannot pretend to forget. He has shown me swords, and now I must choose whether or not to use them. That is what he looks for in my face. My answer. That is what he waits for. Will I use them or not? That is what last night was about. Not about that Roman. Not that I helped drown a man, a single man. Last night was about the fact that I will kill again, at least be expected to kill again. With a sword. With a plan that Carduc has been devising all these years, that my father helped devise before his death. What becomes of us all will be the result of what I say this morning. My choice is nothing less than that. We will take up our swords now, or we never will. We will fight Rome, or we won't. I will accept Rome's treatment of my daughters, or I will not.

Neidriu's foot. Decianus's back.

"Katha, do you know about last night?" I ask. She answers that she does. "And the swords?" She looks to Carduc, then nods. "Who else knows?" I ask Carduc.

"Everyone who has buried a sword knows of theirs, at least."

"How many is that?"

"It's hard to know for sure. Hundreds. Perhaps thousands."

"And all this time, no one spoke of it?" I challenge him.

He smiles. "It's true, at one time that could not have been believed. We were great talkers then, not great keepers of secrets. But when we trusted one another, we had no secrets. Now Rome has fostered distrust, and I believe because of that, silence surrounds the swords. No one knows who has a sword and who doesn't, whom your father considered trustworthy enough to warn and whom he didn't."

He gave me a sword, but he did not consider me trustworthy enough to tell of his plan. I remember wanting to tell him that I did not betray him. Why didn't I tell him? "How many of those who buried swords are still willing to use them, or able for that matter? My father's friends have grown old. How many can be trusted now?" I ask.

"I believe many can be trusted," Carduc answers. "News of what happened in this house has spread. There is rage over Catus Decianus's behavior, and fear, too. If Decianus treats your family this way, what is to stop him from treating others as basely?"

"Perhaps, Carduc, but there are many who have lived comfortably since my father's death, many who have accepted Rome and the tribute. We have resided side by side with them. Friendships have been formed. I have dined at the fort at Flavinus's invitation; he has been our guest. Now I will ask our people to forget these years of peace. Forget these friendships?"

"The peace is broken. And these were never friendships. Was it friendship that brought Decianus to your house? What was done to you and your daughters was done to all of us. The people see that."

"But, even if everyone who buried a sword joined us, Rome can still outnumber us," I retort, knowing already what will happen, knowing at this moment that I will soon carry a sword and ask others to carry theirs. But I must argue against it first, for it is madness to face Rome. I must pretend to believe that there is another way. There must be another way.

"Eventually, yes. But it will take Paulinus time to move his army and even longer for Nero to send more troops from Rome. In the meantime, we have the advantage. Besides, Nero's interest in Britain waxes and wanes. For now, he has found a new amusement that keeps his attention–torturing those who have renounced the Roman gods in favor of a single god."

"I've heard of the worshippers of the one god," I say.

"They die in Nero's arenas for this god they call the one true god."

"They are fools. But you cannot think Nero would be so preoccupied with them that he would turn a blind eye to a rebellion here."

"I think the soldiers are tired of being here. In Rome, they enjoy the sun, and here the dampness works into their bones and their spirits. They have always been afraid here, afraid of our gods, and afraid of spirits who inhabit the land. They believe that at night, if they don't keep guard, these spirits will come and drag them, one by one, into the earth. They want the tin in the east, and they will dig for it, but they know that no matter what they do here the land will never give itself over to them and will never be tamed. And of us–they know us as barbarians, uncivilized and dull-witted, no threat to their empire."

"Maybe so. But what we know of Rome suggests that they do not retreat," I argue. "If we are to take up swords against them, we must be prepared for them to fight back with all their strength."

"Yes, we must be prepared," Carduc agrees.

We will battle Rome. The decision is made though I hardly feel that it is me who made it; it is as though it were made before me, and

I am only its conduit. I have no sense of having chosen, only accepted. "So, we are talking about a rebellion." I do not ask but state it so that we can hear it said aloud. And the words do not fall lightly. Carduc slowly rubs one weathered hand over the other. Katha gets up, goes to one of the jars near the hearth, removes a leaf, goes to another, shakes out some of its contents, rolls the leaf and lights it over the hearth. Coltsfoot, I know it as soon as it starts to burn, but have not smelled it in so long and had forgotten the pleasure and soothing Katha sometimes took from it.

It is difficult for me to conjure any images. The Iceni facing Rome. I cannot envision it. I only see Tallas when I think of rebellion. I see his men fleeing, bolts of blue, see him captured. See Lucius's back.

With a sigh, I dismiss the memory. "We must call the council together," I suggest.

"That would be dangerous." Carduc comes out of his reverie quickly; perhaps it was as discouraging as mine. "There is still an order in effect against our assembling. If the Roman patrollers saw the council members gathering here, there could be suspicion, and repercussions."

"We cannot go any farther without consulting the council. We must at least send for Garan. As the chief council member, he must be consulted."

"Garan is a friend of Rome," Carduc reminds me.

"Of course he is a friend to Rome." My tone derides Carduc. "Prasutagus was a friend to Rome, too. Most of the council is. Otherwise, Rome would have disbanded it. But I have to learn now which of them remembers he is Iceni first, not Roman. I suspect Garan will not remember. Send for Leth, as well. Have him come later. Let me hear what each of them has to say."

———

When Garan arrives, and after Katha has offered him food and drink, he makes it clear that he does not want to speak in front of Carduc. "Leave us, metalworker," he commands with disdain.

"Carduc remains for this meeting," I answer. "He is my advisor, just as he was my father's."

"Yes," Garan accepts reluctantly, "though your husband had no use for his council."

"No, but I remember Carduc sitting at my father's council table; I remember him being listened to. You listened then," I remind him.

Garan throws his head back and smiles scornfully as though the memory is something ridiculous, then announces that he has been to see Flavinus to express the outrage of the tribe on my behalf. I thank him, though it is inappropriate for him to have spoken for me without my consent, spoken for the tribe when he is not king. Now it is my turn to smirk, as it occurs to me that he thinks he is in line for the kingship.

He continues in an officious tone, "Flavinus condemns Decianus's action."

"Does he? What will Decianus's punishment be?" I ask. "Isn't he still sitting in the village collecting debts, making slaves of our people? Is that how Flavinus condemns his action?"

Garan looks as if he is ready with an attempt to defend Flavinus, but I don't give him the opportunity.

"And what of Decianus's threat that all of our territory will be absorbed. All of our territory, Garan. Not just mine–yours as well. All of Iceni territory."

"Rome does not intend to absorb our territory," he answers dismissively.

"No? What do they intend?" I ask. My eyes go over him. He has grown indulgent and soft. At one time, according to stories I have been told, he would have been ostracized for his corpulence, considered a threat to the well being of the tribe in his unwillingness to control his appetite. His silvering moustache is cut short–falling only to his jawline, not extending to his chest in the way my father's did, and his cheeks above the moustache are bloated and blotched.

"They intend to have us go on as we were. We will continue to pay the tribute..."

"They intend," I interrupt him, impatient with his cavalier insistence, "to take everything. Catus Decianus made that clear to me. We cannot go on as we were; we will not be allowed to go on as we were."

"When Paulinus returns here to the east, he will name a new king, someone from the tribe." Garan offers this as though it should allay all my concerns.

"A new king?" I demand. "Not a queen?"

"Forgive me." He bows with insincere respect. "But Flavinus has suggested that the choice will be for a king."

"Would that king be you? Is that what Flavinus has promised?"

"It has been suggested," he answers. "I have been a member of the council since your father was king..."

"I'm aware of your service, Garan. But can't you see that Flavinus is only appeasing you, as he thought he appeased me when he came to offer an apology. But has he arrested Decianus for his treatment of me? Has he driven him out of our territory? The thing that most offends my daughters and me still sits in our village making slaves of our people. Flavinus is clearly impotent. Or complicit. Either way, his promises can't be relied on. He tells us that nothing will change, that as long as we pay tribute we can stay here on our land. Do you hear me? We can stay here on our own land if we only keep paying for the privilege. But the price keeps going up. My daughters, raped. Tribespeople claimed as slaves. Rome is insatiable. And you think you will be king?" Carduc glances warningly at me but Garan deserves my anger, my impudence. "If they wanted you, why weren't you named at my father's death? But maybe you are right. Maybe they will name you king, but only so that they can take that kingship away. You will be king when they claim our land for theirs, when they take us all into slavery. And then, you, the king, will be the first one they turn on. Your wives will be raped before your eyes. Your son, too. And with that sight on your eyes, they will kill you and send you to your next life anguished, disgraced. And you will bear that burden in every life afterward as I will bear the sight of my daughters' agony."

My eyes burn into his, and though I am feeling the exhaustion of this unplanned rant, I am not yet satisfied. "Then when you have died, this is how they will treat your wives." I untie the cord at my waist, remove my dagger-belt, loosen my tunic, then work my arms through it, and let it drop. Naked, I watch his initial lustful excitement dim at the sight of my welted flesh. I touch a sore on the mound of my breast. "This is how the tip of the whip works." I let him gaze, then cover myself.

"Garan," Carduc speaks, "if you believe Rome will name you king, then believe so. Until then, Boudicca assumes her husband's position. It is our way."

Garan nods. "So be it." But there is no conviction in his response. I do not tell him anything of the swords, but I have already said too much, and Garan is clever. "If you do not want things to go on as they are, what is the alternative?"

I do not respond.

"A revolt?" he inquires.

Again, I do not answer.

He considers. "The troops are in the west. There would not be much resistance."

This time I speak. "No, there wouldn't be." He doesn't mention swords, but surely he has one buried somewhere; though I do not trust him, my father would have. We watch each other wondering what the other knows. Perhaps he guesses that there are other swords. Perhaps he thinks that conveying this information to Flavinus will gain him favor. With that thought, I can imagine the digging, the land torn up by Roman hands, the swords discovered, the ruthless consequences. But Garan is not the only clever one here. "But," I remind him cunningly, "no one here, except you, has spoken of revolt."

Fleetingly, his eyes widen. Then his face is immovable. But I saw the terror, just for a moment, that an accusation of plotting against Rome could summon. He is as afraid of them as I am.

"Please keep me informed of any further meetings you have with Flavinus." I bow my head in dismissal of him. "Thank you for coming so quickly."

When he has gone, Carduc worries. "He will be an obstacle. His personal ambition might becloud his judgment. Yet you must form an alliance with him, or he will split the loyalty of the people between you and him. Many will choose not to fight if they see that it is an option embraced by a council member. Unity is critical. Without it, any action we take we will surely fail."

"I will have to offer something," I realize. "He is a man of desires."

"What would satisfy him?"

"I think he is too much like Rome to be satisfied. Nothing will be enough. But I must offer something, anyway."

———

Later, with Leth there is no wariness between us, only bluntness. He was loyal to Prasutagus who was loyal to Rome, but clearly, Leth has never let himself forget that Rome's intentions for us have never been friendly.

"There are swords," he says without hesitation after I have confirmed for him the stories he has heard of the treatment of my daughters and myself, and the plan to annex the entire territory. I do not have to show him my discolored body to persuade him of Rome's malicious intent. "Your father said the swords should stay buried until the right time," he repeats what Carduc has recently reminded me of. "That time is now," Leth ventures.

I regard him. Instead of heavier, like Garan, he has grown thinner in his aging. His body is efficiently built, without excess, perhaps without impressive strength, too, but not yet frail. And he wears his moustaches long, in the old way. Here is an ally, a man I trust, a man our people will trust. Now, with only a nod from me, we will go forward toward rebellion. He watches me; Carduc does, too. "Yes. The time is now," I agree solemnly.

Leth takes a breath. "Do you have trustworthy messengers?"

"Yes."

"I would suggest that you have them spread the word that Rome intends to claim our territory as its own. Tell them that we are all to be made slaves, all our land turned over to Rome. We must incite them. Let them come to the idea of revolt themselves, let them realize, as we have, that it is time to take what swords there are from the ground."

"Yes," I take up this thought. "But by tomorrow we will need to be ready to spread word of a plan. I do not want small rebellions springing up or futile charges made at the fort by impatient tribesmen who have dug up their swords. Tomorrow they must be told to do nothing until they receive word. I will have the messengers warn that any premature action will be treated as a betrayal. No one from the tribe will defend them when Rome captures them. They must wait; we must act as one force."

Because of the respect Leth remembers my father treating Carduc with, he does not bristle as Garan would when Carduc offers a strategy. "The Roman guards have always feared the spirit life of Britain. Since the murdering of the Druids, they fear it more. Perhaps we should begin with the patrollers, one at a time. We will kill them and take the bodies away when possible–into the river, into a hut, if necessary. The disappearances will stir a fear among the survivors. Let them wonder what is becoming of their men. Let them fear their enemy before they know whom that enemy is."

I interrupt. "But we must act quickly. Two nights dealing with patrollers is all we can risk. Suspicion will quickly turn to us. So, we'll start tonight. Tomorrow I'll send messengers to rile the tribe, but once they've dug their swords from the ground, they will want to use them. Three days from now we will have to be ready to give them what they want–the fort. And everyone in it is to be killed. Flavinus included. We must show no mercy."

Leth agrees and adds, "The fort must be burned; we must give the people a visible sign of victory. It will renew their honor and strength. Then we must move on. They will need another target, and we cannot sit here waiting for retaliation."

"Camulodumnum," I suggest. Again, I have the sense that this plan has been laid for me. The course we will take comes to me so clearly. The gods must be speaking to me.

"Yes," Leth grows excited. "Promise them an even greater opportunity for destruction of Roman property. Give them the temple at Camulodumnum–Claudius's temple. We'll send word to the Trinovantes there, advise them that we are coming to return their territory to them.

'We are coming to free you from Roman slavery.' And we will warn them to be ready to join us when we arrive. There we will add another five thousand or more to our number." He pauses, then decides, "The veterans there will not give us much of a fight."

"But by the time we leave Camulodumnum, Paulinus will have received word of the revolt and will be moving east." Carduc's is the voice of fact, cautioning us of the practical truths we need to remember.

But caution is my enemy now; it will only remind me of Rome's strength and of the recklessness of this revolt. This revolt. It is already underway. A day ago I had no thought of it, but now it is planned. "Let Paulinus come," I announce. "The damage to Camulodumnum will already be done. The temple will be destroyed. Rome will know what we think of them and their emperor-gods. Let him come. From Camulodumnum, we will continue south. What Rome has claimed, we will reclaim. From Trinovante territory we will move to Verulamum, stronghold to Roman stronghold, that will be our route."

"Until?" Carduc prods.

He does not mean to discourage me with the question; I believe he asks so that I can say aloud, "Until all the tribes of Britain hear of our conquest and rise up against Rome in their own territories. Until Rome is driven out." I state this as if it is possible, and it must be possible from now on, except in our most private thoughts. And in that privacy which I indulge for just a moment now, I must conceive of a way to protect my daughters if what none of us will mention happens. They must never feel Rome's touch again.

"Leth," I begin. A plan for their rescue is already forming in my head. Is formed. I drive it away. "Forgive me if this offends you as a council member, but issues of propriety must be abandoned at this point. I'll ask you plainly: Can Garan be trusted?"

Carduc seems surprised at my bluntness, but he awaits the answer with curiosity.

"Garan has been a council member since before your father was king," he answers, and I see that he intends to attempt loyalty to the council, and I appreciate it; it is admirable, but we have no time for it.

"Garan believes Rome intends to name him king," I say.

Leth hesitates. "Perhaps not king, but he expects a position."

"A position?"

Again, he lets out a long breath. "When Prasutagus became ill, naturally discussions arose in the council as to who would succeed him. Flavinus assured us that Paulinus would never allow you a position of authority. Forgive me, but they have long memories, and someone involved in a rebellion against them no matter how long ago that was, no matter how young she was, could never be made queen." He looks at me apologetically.

"Go on."

"Flavinus also suggested that changes would be made."

"Changes? Did he suggest the territory would be absorbed? Decianus said that Prasutagus knew? Did he know? Did you know of their plan?"

Leth hesitates. "Flavinus hinted that Rome would take the opportunity to claim the territory. I don't know if he planned to name a king, as such, but positions would be granted to those who would carry out Rome's instructions. According to Flavinus, little else would change. We would stay on the land, but ownership would transfer to Rome. Payment would be made to the Iceni for their service on the land."

"Payment? You believed payment would be made?"

Leth shakes his head. "I don't know what we believed."

"And we'd be working the land for Rome?"

"We work the land for Rome now," he reminds me, "with what we pay in tributes."

"Prasutagus knew."

"He knew that ownership of the land would likely transfer to Rome."

So, he knew. He knew that the arrangement he told me of for our land would not be honored. He knew, and yet, he offered it. And let his family pay the consequences.

Leth is reading the memory of those consequences on my face. He comes to the defense of Prasutagus. "But he couldn't have known what Decianus would do. None of us could."

"And why not? Do we not know what Rome is capable of?"

Leth turns away from my accusing gaze. But I have no interest in blaming him.

"The point is," I continue, "Garan was at these meetings. He knows what Rome's plan is and knows a position might be made available to him. If he wants this position badly enough, he may betray us to Flavinus."

"I do not believe Garan would betray us," Leth argues. "He is a man of ambition, yes, but he is Iceni. However, there will be those who will think our revolt doomed from its conception and who will not risk defying Rome. Garan might be one of those."

"Everyone does not have to join us. They can stand and do nothing and watch the fort burn as long as they do not impede us. Later, I'll ask for volunteers to stay behind. The land has to be tended and protected in our absence. Those who are afraid to join can preserve their honor by offering their services here. Perhaps Garan would like to remain here in the territory. Those who do not join us will need a figure of protection and authority. With Flavinus dead and Paulinus still too far away to have any control, I can name a king. I will give Garan his kingship."

"That may be a solution," Leth answers, "though it may insult him as a warrior to be asked to stay behind."

"On the other hand, if he is unwilling to act against Rome, but still knows himself to be Iceni as you say he does, then this is the only way for him to preserve any honor," I suggest. "And it will preserve the unity of the tribe. Those who don't join us will see that they don't have to join against us."

"I can propose it," Leth offers.

"No, I'll propose it. But you can tell him that a revolt is brewing, that you've heard rumors. When I speak to him, I'll tell him I've heard the rumors, too, and I plan to join. Even if he does inform Flavinus, there won't be enough time for him to mount a defense. Start the attack on the patrollers tonight. Organize a band of tribespeople. Two days from now we will attack the fort. We will gather before dawn, and strike while those in the fort still sleep."

"You don't know yet how many of the tribespeople will join you," Carduc warns.

"No. We won't know until that morning. We could be stopped at the fort if there aren't enough of us to get past the guards. And with patrollers disappearing there are sure to be extra guards assigned."

"As we spread the word of Rome's plan to claim our land," Carduc addresses Leth, "we should also remind people of the abuses Rome has committed against them. We must, all of us, remember every mistreatment. It will be those memories, the individual hatreds that will fan the spirit for battle. The welfare of the tribe, the reclamation of our land are both worth fighting for and should be fought for. But in the end, we must fight for ourselves; each one must give the struggle her own meaning." He looks to me.

Leth agrees, then grins, "It will be good to carry a sword again." He pats his right hip where the sword will hang. "You have given us back our swords, Boudicca. Your father would be proud."

I am glad to earn my father's pride, and it is wonderful to think of Leth with his sword, but I am thinking of what Carduc said. It *should* be for the sake of the tribe that I fight, for the tribe and for Icenia that I face Rome, but it is for my own revenge. Had Decianus not done what he did, I would not have been able to summon the will or the courage to even conceive of such an uprising. Now I am to lead it. The Druids were massacred; I did not think of rebellion. I did nothing to relieve the burden of my tribespeople's tributes because the tribute was not such a burden for me. Now, though, because I have suffered, I act, and expect them to act with me. They will not follow. Why should they?

But this doubt is for that private place in me, the same place that holds my plan for rescuing my daughters if our revolt fails.

Before Leth leaves, I spit out the name, "Decianus. He is the only one I want taken from the fort alive." Leth waits to hear my plan for revenge, but I do not know yet what my intentions are.

When Leth has gone, with my daughters on my mind, I ask Carduc to collect some herbs for me. "Wormwood and hops." He knows how I will use them; I can see that in his face— sorrow. But I match his gaze with determination, the determination of a mother willing to do what she must to protect her children.

NINETEEN

It is good that we will act quickly. No time to lose resolve. I do wish there were an alternative. I wish that because I am afraid, and I am ashamed of that fear. Still, I wish there were another way. But there is no other way. There never was one. We have been moving inexorably toward this since Rome, in the person of Julius Caesar, first tramped on Britain. It was he who determined this rebellion long before I was even born. It is he who determined this destiny for me.

The girls know their first afternoon of utter distraction since the day our home was invaded. Though alarmed by the news that we will be attacking the fort, the chores they are assigned of preparing a bundle of extra clothing for themselves, and of ripping and winding strips of cloth for bandages keep them busy. But winding bandages is the smallest of their duties. Their work also is in the way they glance so frequently at me, the way they so unabashedly look and find reassurance, protection in my presence. They serve as reminders to me of what Rome will take if I lose heart and think too long about alternatives to this rebellion. They are what will keep me steadfast; they will demand from me the courage I need to protect them.

At night they sleep beside me again. Why should I force them into their own beds when they'll be abandoning those beds for the back of a wagon or the hard ground in just two days?

We will be in the midst of it in two days. And what is happening in the woods now? How many patrollers are having their heads held down in the river? How many are turning with a gasp to find Iceni eyes on them? An Iceni sword–impossible, they must think–cutting the darkness just before it cuts their flesh. Good. How many heads are bouncing to the ground, how many chests have been opened? Yet, here there is quiet. Over the rhythmic breathing of my daughters' sleep I strain to hear the sound of Roman death, but I hear nothing. Is it happening? Could Leth not gather enough tribespeople to ambush the patrollers? Is our plan already abandoned? Or worse, was it attempted and quashed–Iceni dead in the woods, Rome alerted? Where is the noise of death?

All night I listen for it.

Morning comes, and it is long, as the night was, with waiting, with wondering. My sleeplessness undermines my resolve and provokes a deep sense of vulnerability. Rome feels close. And angry. I advise the girls to hide the bandages and instruct Katha and Leanan to finish the preparations discretely.

Twice I step out into the yard, but no one is riding in. If our warriors failed, if the Roman patrollers are still alive, there will be brutal retaliations. I send guards out to check the roads. If any Romans are spotted coming this way I will be here when they arrive, but my daughters will not. The route I took with Carduc into the woods, that is the way I will send them. Through the fields to the woods with Katha and Leanan. "Do not come back," I will tell them. "Do not ever come back."

Finally, an Iceni rider comes–a messenger from Leth.

The ambush was successful. All night, while I heard nothing, Roman patrollers were being dragged deep into the woods and their bodies made to disappear. Silent killings. And now the plan will go forward. A day from now, in the predawn darkness, we will attack the fort.

Later in the morning, Garan comes to see me. I tell him of the plan as though it is something put in motion by its own force. "Word has spread of what happened here in this house, and what Rome intends to do with our land. Our people have given Rome as much as they are willing and able to give. Now Rome has broken the trust, and our people will defend themselves and their property. Rumors abound of a rebellion," I tell him. "I, too, will defend myself and what is mine, and I will offer myself as the leader of the rebellion. Our people need a leader." I pause, then remind him of what he pointed out to me. "Paulinus is too far away to stop us. And we outnumber the Romans here and in Camulodumnum."

"This is rash." He shakes his head. "Rome is not our enemy." He seems to search for a solution, but finds none. "What will they use as weapons?" he asks as though he does not know the answer.

I wait, letting him realize that we both know it is a game he plays. "There are swords, Garan," I say plainly. "You know that. Surely my father advised you of that. Your own sword is buried somewhere."

His eyes move as he thinks. If my father did not tell him, Garan would not reveal that now. To have been so distrusted as to be excluded from my father's confidence would be too shameful for Garan to admit.

"And there are likely many more swords at the fort," I add. "But, I think that even without swords, this rebellion would go on."

"How many will join the revolt?" he asks, tracing one side of his moustache with a finger.

"Many," I answer, as though I could be sure.

He scowls, perhaps realizing that there is no use in informing Flavinus because then he would have to stand with Flavinus against his own people. And that he will not do, though his resentment for this forced loyalty is apparent.

Now I will see if I can bait him. "But some villagers will need to stay behind to tend to the fields and the herds. And to protect the land here."

The sound of his labored breathing fills the space between us.

"Those who stay behind will need a strong leader with them," I suggest, "someone from the council whose authority they will respect. Someone who would essentially serve as king." I will not name him and risk, as Leth warned, insulting the warrior–if there still is one–in him.

He nods, as though he is considering carefully the candidates for this position. But guided by his cowardice and his avarice, I am confident that he will suggest himself for the role. *King*, he is surely thinking now, *and once king, wouldn't I remain as such?* It is a risk to give him a role he will not want to relinquish, but it is a safer than risking his siding against me and trying to divide the tribe.

Visits with him are exhausting, and when he leaves there is nothing to do but wait and sleep. And wait again. Wait for night. Wait for morning. And then night again. Wait to do what should never be done.

It comes quietly, the last night on which Rome's actions will go unanswered. The last night when my daughters will go unavenged. Quiet night. It follows afternoon and evening, coming the way every other night does. And like other recent nights it brings loneliness–a hollowing loneliness. Even with my girls on either side, I am lonely. "It gives me courage," I told Grawnei of my father's sword. So, I slip my legs out from under Neidriu's and dig it up, wanting some of its gift. I hold it, as I used to so often with Carduc. But my strength is gone, and I can keep the blade tilted upward for only a short time. Longer. Longer, I demand of myself, but I am weak. And the sword proves not to be the company I need; my loneliness is only worsened by my discouraging lack of strength. I bury the sword once more. "Tomorrow you will be released from your grave," I promise it. Pulling the mat over the carelessly covered spot, I arrive at a way to provide myself companionship. Instinctual, this solution must be offered from somewhere deep in my body–strange because my memory has not held a thought of this item in so long.

Quietly, I open the chest where clothes and blankets and a small jewelry chest are kept. Prasutagus's bracae are there, and an old cloak of his. But I do not want to miss him now, and quickly put those items aside, and lift others out of the chest until I find the thing I seek. My wedding cloak. Folded over. I lay it on the ground next to me and repack the trunk. Then carrying the cloak, I climb back over Neidriu into the bed. Now I turn my full enjoyment to the cloak, its color drained by age and darkness, but I know its shades. I unfold it, hold it to my face, and remember everything. Tallas.

Before dawn I awaken in bed from a half-sleep, the cloak, like a blanket, pulled to my chin.

Katha recognizes it when she enters a little later. "The old cloak," she says, taking up a handful of it from the end of the bed, and examining it. "It's faded, but still the color of..."

124

I expect her to say "Tallas's eyes," and I almost finish the thought for her, but she surprises me. "Grawnei's eyes," she says, smiling. She has never asked me about Grawnei's father, and I have never said anything of it. But I see now, that of course she knew all along, knew from the moment of Grawnei's birth, as I suspected she did. I smile with her.

"I'll wear it," I tell her.

She nods, then urges me out of bed, and I let her comb my hair the way she used to. "Still so thick," she says as the teeth of the comb catch.

"Though like the cloak, a little faded." I remember Tallas touching it for the first time. Then it was bright. And Prasutagus wanting a bracelet of it–then it was already dull.

"Still lovely." Katha works out every snarl, until my scalp tingles with her vigor and my hair lies smoothly down my back. Then she turns her attention to waking the girls.

I open the chest again and remove the jewelry box. My mother's torque. Broken vow. I will make no more vows; then I will break no more vows. The gold closes around my neck, cool in its still familiar way. I find my bracelets, gold and enameled red and blue.

Katha helps to get Grawnei and Neidriu dressed, though they could dress themselves. All the while she coos and chatters, calming and reassuring them, distracting them from the day's deeds to come. Yet all the while I know she worries, and so she gives her hands and her voice over to the fretting–cooing and arranging–and Neidriu and Grawnei respond warmly to it as I always have. I expect to be able to return home after the attack on the fort, before we start for Camulodumnum, and so could leave them here until then. But they should witness this attack; their eyes and their memories must hold the revenge that is taken in their names. They must see the men who raped them burned to know that their ordeal is truly over.

With them watching, I retrieve my sword, again, from the ground, exercise my arms with it for a few moments, oil it, replace it in its scabbard, then belt it under my cloak. So unaccustomed am I to the weight of it pulling at my hip, the length of it against my leg, that I must stand in place for several moments, finding my balance. And when I do first walk with it, it is awkwardly, leaning to the left to accommodate the bulk on the right. But quickly the weight becomes familiar again, remembered by my body despite the years without it.

Grawnei watches me closely. I almost think she wants to offer a suggestion, advise me on a posture. But she says nothing and silently straps the dagger and belt that Carduc made for her under her cloak. Neidriu does the same.

Outside, Carduc greets me. He has dressed the chariot and the pony regally. At his side is a sword. At the sides of the guards who will accompany us are swords. On them, the weapons seem natural, so natural that they have already learned how to use their bodies to ballast the weight. Carduc presents me with a helmet of great ornamentation. He must have been working on it for months, surely well before this rebellion was decided on. A bird sits atop it–hawk-like, hungry, large-beaked, wings rising. And a new shield, though I have my own–the Romans saw no need to confiscate those when they disarmed us.

With a dozen guards riding ahead, we set, slowly, out. I ride alone in my chariot; Carduc rides alongside me, leading a calf that will be sacrificed at the fort. Katha and my daughters ride behind in another chariot, Leanan, horsed, alongside them. More guards follow, along with a number of field workers and herders, though I had Carduc advise them to wait to join us until after the fort was taken. If we fail, though I doubt I can protect anyone of us from Rome's retribution, I would like to think the consequences would not be as severe for those who did not participate. But I will not deny these people the honor of joining us in the overtaking of the fort, if that is an honor they are willing to pay consequences for. All the way we are on alert for patrollers, and are wary of ambush. Garan may betray us still, but I am prepared to kill him if I must. It would be an unpropitious first battle-Iceni against Iceni, the first blood drawn by me with my father's sword from that of his council member. But if I must, I will. A friend to Rome is an enemy to me. There can be no exceptions.

We move slowly, but my mind works hectically, abandoning Garan now for memories of my father, of the silent ride I took with him through the dawn of my wedding day. "Father, I did not betray you," I say in this memory. "I knew nothing of Tallas's rebellion." And he nods at me. No, he never nodded that morning. We were silent and our eyes did not meet. I glance to Carduc who is slowed by the clumsy calf.

No patroller stops us; we reach the village safely. Carduc lets out a low whistle and the guards up front stop, as does the rest of our procession. In a short distance the fort will be visible, and if there are Roman guards left alive, we will be visible to them.

Leth appears, and with him come only four men. But there are others in the darkness. Many others. Quick shadows draw my eyes–crouched figures darting between the huts. Iceni. And, there. A flash of bright white. Before my mind can read it, my body remembers a sight from long ago–blue–and it triggers a shudder. But this, now, is not a warrior running in defeat, as my body has warned me. This is not Tallas's battle of so many years ago. This is not a warrior abandoned by his courage, but a warrior full of bravery, his hair limed and spoked so that it is like a bright wheel on his head. And there, there is another–streaked blue and naked except for leather belts crisscrossing his waist, and shafts of iron riding his hip. That twittering, no, it is not a bird's call but a signal, being passed and picked up; the village is bristling.

Leth takes a proffered conch from one of his men, and he holds it out to me. "We cannot go into battle silently," he says.

I had imagined us going silently, surrounding the fort, surprising the Romans and giving them no opportunity to defend themselves. But that is only because it has been so long since I thought of my people as warriors, since I remembered how we entered battle: fiercely and with fierce cries. And that was how it would be tonight.

The twittering ceases; the night becomes still. Now there is just the snorting of the horses, and our breathing. My daughters' faces shine in the darkness; their terror is bright.

"The sacrifice, first," I say, dismounting the chariot.

Habit has my hand going to my dagger but Carduc catches my eye and the hand moves to the other hip. I pull at my sword, careful to make the unsheathing of it a smooth, single motion. Once it is freed from its scabbard, I hold it above my head with both hands, its tip aimed at the night, its blade lighting the darkness–a thin iron flame.

"Apollo-Belinus, Teutates, Taranis, Esus, Epona, Minerva, Icena– accept this offering with our praise. Let its blood please you, and if you are satisfied, protect us in this imminent battle. Give us the strength to send these oppressors back across the sea. Help us to cleanse our land, your land of these invaders. Great rider goddess, Epona, guide our horses. Minerva, quench our thirsts when we bring them to your streams. Icena, soon the blood of this calf will soak into the land that is you. But it is nothing. The blood of Rome will saturate this land. Accept it and forgive us for letting Roman boots trod on you. Andraste, goddess of the fight, see this calf. A small gift. Ignite us with your ferocity, and bodies and blood will be yours."

With a grunt, I bring the blade down onto the neck of the calf. Its legs fold. The blood on my blade is bright, and I raise the sword again for all to see. A bloody sword. Sacrificial blood.

When I have sheathed the sword, Neidriu dismounts and runs to me. Trembling, she takes my hand and pulls.

"Yes," I answer to her need for ritual. "Grawnei," I call. "Come." We circle the calf three times, and I pray once more. "See these daughters, protect them."

Katha returns them to the chariot; I take the conch from Leth, and am about to put it to my mouth when a hare dares to investigate the bloodied ground. Stealthily, Leth crouches behind it, and snatches it by its scruff.

"Perhaps it is sent by the gods," he says, extending the animal toward me. I take the hare- -all twitches and fur–and hold it to myself, then let it leap. It bolts to the east. What it means, I do not know; that we should head east? But we must go south.

Leth offers no interpretation; nor does Carduc.

I step back onto the chariot and put the conch to my lips. Its sound is mournful, but it brings the night acutely alive. My call is met with screams and shrieks, and in every direction there is movement. Forward. "Forward." Now the fort becomes visible but my eyes are drawn past it to bouncing lights in the near woods. Torches. There. And there. More. Iceni emerging from behind trees. Hundreds.

Luminous hair. Glint of metal. Rocks begin soaring over the palisades that surround the fort, pelting the soldiers in the yard.

Carduc signals our party to halt, but Leth rides ahead to join the charge.

"Decianus," I call to him.

He waves his hand at me in acknowledgment and rides on.

Carduc stays behind and orders guards to close in around the chariots. My participation in this battle is to be limited. I am to remain uninjured for as long as possible. A maimed queen, a dead queen inspires little confidence. "You must stay alive," Carduc has advised me. "You are the impetus behind this revolt. Once Rome kills you, they will believe they have killed the heart of the tribe. It will fortify them and dishearten the Iceni. You must not be impulsive."

And doesn't that suit me? Isn't this a cowardice that keeps me from running into the yard of the fort now in defiance of Leth's and Carduc's suggestion? Who are they to direct a queen's actions? What prevents me from assisting my tribesman who is there–I can see him through the gate that has been forced open–struggling against a Roman? Why don't I go? There, at last, he swings his sword.

The Roman guards offer resistance. Even with the unexpectedness of the attack, even though the sounds of the conch and the scream-ing must have sent shivers through them, they are undaunted. Their perpetual preparedness–this they will always have in their favor, the training that makes them soldiers, always ready, while we will have to rely, not on training, but on anger. Even now when the Romans can hardly know whom it is that they battle, they fight well. "Who are these wild men and women?" they may ask themselves. "Iceni, but how? They have no swords." Yet they overcome their confusion and give battle.

I will go now. To the fort. Now. That Roman. There. I will kill him from behind. Carduc will prevent me. I will go anyway. Now. But wait, a flow of Iceni into the yard, villagers who have heard the cries. Through the gate, over the walls. More. Hundreds more. Quickly the advantage is ours. Long swords swing at their targets, finding their marks before the Romans can step in close enough with their short swords to offer much defense. Shrieking. The hard and unfamiliar clang of swords on swords.

Then a growing quiet. And from my position, the activity ceases. Through the gate, I see bodies, motionless, fallen. Quiet. Then muffled sounds from within the fort. And a screech, so sudden and shrill, it jolts me. A signal, I realize as torches hurtle through the night, spiraling flames onto the roof of the fort. Leth has coordinated this battle well.

Our party strains forward.

Now there is no quiet. Iceni run from the fort. Cheering. Shouting. Flames spike the sky, lick their way down the sides of the fort, spark and burst. No Romans come running. All of them—dead? My eyes tell me it is true, but I cannot trust anything Roman, especially Roman defeat. Yet no Romans come running.

Then from the rear of the fort exits a prisoner, naked and unarmed. He is not bound, but the sword tips poking at him serve as shackles.

Catus Decianus. I know it before I can see the face. Hunched. Fleshy. Decianus. My fury is instant. "Neidriu. Grawnei," I call harshly. Carduc delivers them from their chariot to mine. "Look," I say when they are next to me, and I order a guard out of the way so they can see Decianus approaching. "Do you see him?" Neidriu presses against me. "No," I scold her, pushing her away. "Stand and look at him. Show him no fear. Look into his face. He cannot hurt you." Then to the guards, I command, "Open the circle." Leth and the three other captors bring Decianus into our midst, then the guards move in again, surrounding him.

Filth. He lifts his eyes to me; I see past his scorn to his fear. Now, Leth pricks him with the sword. "Kneel," he demands. "Kneel," and prods him again. Decianus's flesh answers with blood. He drops on his knees.

Neidriu shivers at my side; Grawnei is rigid. "He will not hurt you," I assure them loudly so that he hears, too. "Never again."

"Beg forgiveness from the queen," Leth commands.

Decianus says nothing; Leth swipes his shoulder with his sword.

Now the Roman wretch cries out, holding his wound. "Be merciful," he begs. "I acted for Nero."

This coward. Craven and obsequious now. But then. Then...And there was no mercy. He watches. What words should I spit at him? But words are so insufficient. And why should I let him hear my anguish? Let him go to his death knowing my pain? Let him see me cry in rage? No. Words cannot serve me; they are flimsy in the face of this. What he will know are my cold eyes, my set face, the mercilessness of my silence.

I signal toward the yard, wanting a greater audience for this deed than the small circle here. Leth understands, and he and his men lead Decianus.

I only regret that I do not have hammer and spike, for I would nail him to the gate the way Tallas was nailed to the tree. Still, cords of leather will serve, and I instruct my guards to tie him, wrist and wrist to the gate. I stand before him now as he struggles to free himself.

This will not be the first man I kill. He will not be the last.

I draw my sword, hoist it with two hands into the sky, and with a grunt, thrust it downward with the entirety of my strength. It finds the already pierced shoulder and opens it more deeply, but misses the head I wanted to cleave. Blood. His legs collapse but the leather ties hold him, slumping. Better that I missed. I want the head whole, I decide, and now I bring the blade around, sideways. At his neck. One motion. The weight of the sword leading me. His head flies away from his body, drops and rolls in the dirt. The neck sputters blood. "The head," I shout, my fury still full. And to another guard, "A spear or a post. Break a post from the gate. Spike the head." The guards enthusiastically oblige, and the head is shoved violently on its stake, and triumphantly handed to me.

Carduc nods. Whether he follows my train of thought, or I follow his, I do not know which, but at this signal, I remount my chariot. "Take the reins," I instruct Grawnei.

"Clear the way," Carduc yells.

"Take us around the fort," I instruct Grawnei. Obediently, she cracks the pony's back, and we start around in a sun-wise direction outside the enclosure of the burning fort. Our people will hardly make way; instead they want to be near, cheering my daughters and me, celebrating the sight of Decianus's head, and Grawnei cannot bring the pony to a gallop though the rage of the kill is still in me and a gallop is what I want. The rush of the blood in my ears is forced to ebb; the heaving of my chest slows. Neidriu stands between Grawnei and me, away from my stake, and I become aware again of her shivering. On the second trip around I notice Garan. Now that the work is done and no Roman is left alive to accuse us, accuse him, he has joined our party in the yard of the fort. On the third circumnavigation, I pray, "Accept the Romans of this fort as an offering for our victory." Victory. I feel the tumult in me waning, feel the rage give way to fatigue and sorrow. Why sorrow? Not for what I have done. I have no regret. But then why sorrow?

Katha takes the girls from my chariot, wraps them in the warmth of herself. With the fire still burning, and the dawn giving way to morning, I lean my hideous stake against the gate of the fort–a salute to my people, and a greeting for Paulinus who will surely descend on us once word of our deeds travels.

TWENTY

Two Romans dead at my hands. And they are only the first. There is more blood to shed. I have decided that now for all of us. Even for those who will not join me, I have decided for them. There will be more blood, and there is no turning back from that.

Tomorrow, at dawn, we will set out for Camulodumnum. Today there is reveling and looting of what is left of the fort. Many of our swords are found and recovered; many Roman weapons are confiscated, as well. So we have back what is ours, and have taken from them what they once took from us.

I would like to move on, but both Carduc and Leth caution patience; the tribe must be allowed to enjoy its victory. "How long has it been since there was no Roman in this territory?" Leth asks me. "How long since the village was truly ours?"

In our house, we do not celebrate. Killing Decianus has not ameliorated my anger but fed it. I see his death, and I think of his deeds. There is no satisfaction in that. And despite Leth's protestations, the destruction of the fort does not give us victory, not with Paulinus's army within marching distance of us.

Grawnei's silence is no less intractable; witnessing the killing of Decianus has brought her no closer to speaking. In her silence she must wonder what world this is where soldiers, soldiers who were called here long ago to protect us, rape, and a mother parades with a head on a stick. Yes, I am the same mother, Grawnei, who has combed your hair so gently and let you comb mine. But I am someone else, too. And Neidriu. She prays and will only eat a small portion of what Katha gives her to eat or drink. The rest she offers to the gods. They watch me as though they don't dare to take their eyes away, as though they can no longer be sure of what I will do, no longer be sure that I can be the mother they knew.

But I am their mother, fierce mother, and with that ferocity, I have avenged them. And with that ferocity, I have frightened them.

Leanan sees their horror and feels compelled to assuage it. She brings them the pups even though it is too soon for them to be weaned from their mother; it bodes badly for the pups' futures. But I do not refuse; the girls are cheered, and it will be good for them to have something to care for in the days to come, something to nurture while their fearsome mother hacks and kills.

Now the hacking and killing must be planned.

"It will take two days to reach Camulodumnum," Leth anticipates, after he has returned to me from visiting his wives. Both wives–sisters––lost babies at their births, but children have come and gone through their home, sick children who could not be cured in their own homes have been restored to health in the care of Leth's wives. That the sisters' children could not be saved is the price the gods exacted from them for their gifts of healing. So two babies died, and many children lived, and the village has always been grateful for their sacrifice. "Tonight we should send riders ahead to inform the Trinovantes that we are coming and give them time to prepare to join us."

"That may also give the veterans there time to prepare or flee if anyone of them hears anything of it," Carduc warns.

"They will not flee," I suggest. "Their arrogance will not allow them to flee. They will believe they can overcome us. And what preparations can they make? If this morning is an indication of how many tribespeople will join us, the veterans will be too outnumbered for their preparations to make any difference. They cannot get another troop there before we arrive. Can they?"

"I don't see how," Leth answers, an equivocal response. We are too well trained in Rome's capabilities to discount any possibility.

I assume a tone of defiance, "I don't see how, either. Still, instruct the riders to be careful, and have them spread the word among the Trinovantes that a *small* band of Iceni is coming. That will be what the veterans hear, if they hear anything. Then have the messengers leave the village and wait. The next day, they will go back, and they will tell the Trinovantes that our numbers have swelled. This time, when there is even less chance of the veterans being able to prepare themselves for us, the messengers can be a little less careful. Let the old Romans hear something of the plan. Let them know we are on the way. Thousands of us. I want the scent of fear on them when we arrive."

"Fear can make them brutal," Carduc warns. "We must be prepared for a struggle."

"We are prepared," I retort. But of course, he is right. It was the fear of the Druids that made Paulinus so vicious toward them, and the fear of the spirits' of the Druids that made Seneca and Decianus so vicious to us. Still, I will take the risk; I want to know they feared our coming. I want them to know hopelessness.

"Will you ride with the head of Catus Decianus tomorrow?" Leth asks. "Let that news precede us, also. 'The Iceni are led by Queen Boudicca who carries the head of the tribute collector on her staff.'"

He had become *my* enemy. But Catus Decianus was hateful to many, I remember. My bitterness toward him has been so singular that I have not considered the atrocities he's committed against others--the relentless collection of tributes, the confiscation of property, the enslavements.

"His head on a pole is a welcome sign that we have thrown off the burden of the Roman tribute," Leth persuades me.

The tribute. I hadn't thought of it until now but the paying of tributes is over. What freedom that must feel like today for those who have struggled to make their payments. But Decianus, I want to be rid of him, though his head on a stick is a sure device for inciting action. "Retrieve it," I decide. "But keep it away from my house, and away from my daughters. I do not want his eyes on them. In the morning I will ride into the village displaying it. We will carry it as far as

Camulodumnum. After that I want no more to do with him. He is not a companion I want with me in this battle."

"I will remove the eyes," Carduc offers, "and soak the head in cedar oil to preserve it for the ride."

"What is left of it," I point out. "It may be being kicked around the yard of the fort right now. I hope it is."

Not satisfied that the plan has been thoroughly reviewed, Carduc presses ahead, "And what, after Camulodumnum?"

I look to Leth. "Verulamum," I say. "We decided on Verulamum. It is the next closest Roman village."

Leth agrees.

"And then?" Carduc asks.

"We've decided all this, Carduc," I remind him, impatiently. "From Verulamum to Londinium."

"And then?" he persists.

Is he challenging me? My decisions? My authority? My capabilities? Why do his questions always sound as though they mean to challenge me? "What do you want to know, Carduc?"

"What are you afraid of?"

"Afraid of?" I demand. "Do I show fear? Or do I sound afraid?" I look to Leth who seems as perplexed as I am.

"Think about tomorrow," Carduc urges me quietly. "Think about tomorrow."

"Carduc..."

"What worries you? What do you see? Close your eyes and think about tomorrow, what would you see?"

"I will not close my eyes." But now he has closed his. And sees tomorrow? What does he see? And Leth. Now, he is staring down at the table, thinking, seeing? What? With a sigh of exasperation, I put my hand to my eyes and cover them. At first, I can only think of how Carduc has irritated me. And how his question is so foolish. What am I afraid of? I am afraid of Rome. I am afraid of not being able to protect my daughters. I am afraid of death. Afraid of defeat. Afraid of all the killing I will do. Afraid those Iceni who attacked the fort will think their work is done and will not join us tomorrow. I open my eyes.

"What good is this exercise, Carduc?" I ask. "I have fears, why should I entertain them the night before we set out for battle?"

"How can you assuage those fears?" he asks.

"We can defeat Rome, and then my fear will be assuaged. Then there will be no more fear." But he is not satisfied, and now, I spitefully oblige him. My fears have been raised. Let him share them with me. "The burning of the fort is meaningless unless we continue our actions throughout the east, and throughout the entire island. Otherwise, Rome will only find replacements for the men we killed at the fort, and our past tributes will be meager compared to the punishment they will mete out. We will be taken as slaves. Or killed." I consider. "You ask what I am afraid of. What if I do not get the number of people I need to join me? What if some feel that the burning of the fort and the killing of the Romans here is enough? What if they say that Camulodumnum is Trinovante territory, and so it is the Trinovantes to free? But," I argue, more with myself than with Carduc, "they must know we cannot stay here, doing nothing, waiting for Rome to take revenge. Still, some may say that we have done our part, and now others should do theirs. We need others to join us. We can't rid the entire island of Romans by ourselves."

"The Trinovantes will join." Leth is sure.

"Yes. But others must join as well," I realize. "All the tribes. We must fight as one. That is the only true way to win this war, all of us sharing the victory as we shared the abuses. Rome cannot fight us all. That has been their advantage: the divisiveness among us, our bickering for territory. But if we united, all against Rome, we would be unassailable. Then Rome would run for their ships and never return."

"The tribes have never united," Leth muses, not without hope.

"We have never had a common enemy," I say.

"Not all see Rome as an enemy," he reminds me.

"Not all. But since their attack on the Druids many more have come to regard Rome with suspicion, at least."

"Yes, but that suspicion which is really fear may be just what keeps them from joining us; it may even push them to join Rome in an attempt to protect themselves."

"But there will be others who will want a way to fight back; we offer a way," I say. "Some may be afraid to act on their own but not afraid to act with us. We must do whatever we can to gain an advantage. Rome will do what they can."

"They will," Leth answers gravely. "But when we spread word of our revolt even if it is to invite assistance, we risk discovery of our plan by Romans in every territory."

"Everything we do is risky. And remember, their army is still in the west. Most of the territories are settled like Trinovante territory, with veterans. Paulinus has the majority of the soldiers with him, with some small units scattered in the south and in the north. I'll send messengers. We have to at least attempt unity, and perhaps those who don't join us here can start incursions of their own." I am thinking quickly now, hopefully, strategically. It seems possible to me that we could unite. It must be possible. "We'll also need a network of scouts. I need to be able to receive word quickly of the movement of any Roman troops, especially of Paulinus's army. Establish a system where news can be passed from territory to territory, on to me. Choose riders who are swift and discerning. They will need to determine the trustworthiness of the other tribes. If they hear of factions that are friendly toward Rome, then they must ride on and not risk inviting that tribe to join us who may instead join against us. Send messengers into Catuvellauni territory. The Coritani to the west will join. Go south into Cantiaci territory, and to the Atrebates. The Silures in the west have always distrusted Rome, but they will prefer to fight on their own. However, send word anyway. Alert them to the fact that Paulinus will be moving his army toward us. Perhaps the Silures can provide some interference with the furtive poisonings of food supplies and hobbling of Roman horses that I've heard they are so adept at."

"The Dobunni may send a troop," Leth suggests.

"And the Demetae, but they are so far west. Avoid the Brigantes in the north. Cartimandua turned over her own husband to Rome for the sake of a client-queenship," I remind Leth. "Let those who want to join us know that they cannot delay. We will be moving quickly."

Leth concurs.

Carduc has listened silently. Now I ask him, "What do you think?"

"It is a good plan," he reflects.

"It is a good plan," I repeat, "and I would not have thought of it unless you prodded me. Why didn't you simply suggest it, Carduc?"

"I had not thought of trying to unite the tribes. You thought of it. I only asked you what you feared. You must know as much about your fears as you can before you go into battle. To be surprised by them in the midst of the fighting will be to be undone by them."

I look at him now and know that if I can be patient and trusting enough to tolerate his questions, he will find a way to unleash in me all the answers that I will need, even answers that I might wish could have remained unknown.

With our plan determined, there is nothing to do but rest, and I am tired. Again, I pull the wedding cloak over me and look at it for a reminder of Tallas's eyes. Can you see me? Tallas, I speak to you, and yet I do not see you. I cannot form your face clearly. Why do Prasutagus's features come when I want to recall your face? Forgive me. I know your eyes. I know your dark hair. I know Lucius's back blocking your face from mine. And now I will go on with the killing. Did you think I could? What would you think of me, now, your bloody-handed Boudicca? Where is your face? Your face, our daughter's voice. Rome will give these things back to me. I will kill until I have gotten them back. But that is a vow, and I want no more vows. But I will. I will kill until I can see your face and until Grawnei speaks.

In the morning, for the first time in years, I wake to the sight of a sword–my father's sword, my sword. I did not bury it last night but let it rest against the wall within reach if I needed it. So aloof, it seems, so removed from me, there, and not in my hand. But it is a part of me now as surely as killing is part of me. The enamels of the scabbard reclaim their colors from the darkness as Katha stokes the fire in my room.

"It's warm enough," I say quietly. "The cold weather is over."

"Ah, let the girls wake to a fire. Who knows how long it will be before they wake here again."

"At least the time of year won't be against us," I say. "We won't have the cold and ice to worry about."

"No, but there will be rains," she comments.

"Some," I concede.

She turns from the fire, looks down at the basket the pups are lying in at the side of the bed, and snaps her tongue at the roof of her mouth.

"Katha?"

She faces me. "Those pups shouldn't be away from their mother."

I cannot keep myself from letting out a quiet laugh. "On this morning, of all mornings, you're worried about pups?"

"The well-being of the animals should not be risked for the sake of indulging children," she reprimands me, her voice rising. I hear the tension in it, the apprehension that is not for the pups. "If the pups die, it'll be worse for the girls than if they never had them at all."

"Then see that they don't die, Katha," I say as matter-of-factly as I can.

She puts her hands on her hips, and I know I will be getting a scolding. "Boudicca, you know I have enough to do and enough heads to protect and mouths to feed without worrying about two pups on top of it all."

I smile. "Katha, you take care of things. That is what you do. It is your nature. Look how you've taken care of me." I put my arms around her, and am surprised at the small shudderings of her shoulders. "Are you crying?" I ask.

"But I can't take care of you, anymore," she answers.

No, she can't. I have moved outside the realm of her protection; I have moved beyond the safety of her arms.

I rub my palm up and down her back. "Don't be afraid," I whisper. "I can't hide my fear when I see yours. And when you cry, I cry."

"Tears don't make you weak, remember," she states decidedly, wiping my cheeks with her thumbs. Then turning away, she adds, "And I'm not afraid," and she is all efficiency again as she goes to the bed to wake the girls.

I dress.

"Where is Little Tail?" Neidriu asks before she is fully awake. Little Tail is one of the names she calls her pup. "Pup" is another.

"There," Katha answers, "in the basket with her sister." Then over her shoulder to me, she adds, "They whimpered half the night. Didn't you hear them? I did." She turns to Grawnei who is sitting up now. "And your pup still needs a name." The silence worries Katha, though she pretends to be patient. "She will speak again," she's assured me, "as soon as something else occupies her thoughts. What is in her thoughts now is not anything she wants to say." And yet, I believe Katha secretly hopes that it will be to her that Grawnei will finally speak. And so each day, she provides Grawnei with an opportunity to respond.

"Perhaps she's already given her pup a name," I suggest. And I would like it to be me that Grawnei chooses as the recipient of her recovered voice. Yet, somehow I suspect I will be among the last to hear it. "But for now it's a secret. Maybe that's what we should call her pup, then. 'Secret.' Is that all right, Grawnei?" She looks into my face, and I into hers, but I can read nothing there, and I am not as good as Katha is at pretending patience. The silence disturbs me deeply, and the longer it goes on, the more it seems to threaten her and us, the more it seems to bode something, something that can't be good. It is Rome's power over her. Rome continuing to exert its power. And if I can't overcome that in my own home, with my own daughter, how can I expect to succeed in overthrowing their power outside this house? If she continues to succumb to them, doesn't that mean they are still among us? Doesn't that mean others will succumb? And now I have promised. Her voice. His face. I will have them. "How long will you let Rome keep your tongue?" I ask. "Why do you give them even more than they take?"

Of course, she does not answer.

"Speak, Grawnei." I take her by the shoulders. "Speak."

She does not.

"Speak." Now I shake her. "What is this killing worth if you keep Rome alive in your heart? What will it take, Grawnei? A hundred killings? A thousand?" She will cry at any moment; the tears are already in her eyes. But she won't let me see them fall. Stubborn girl. "Stubborn girl."

A quick glance at Neidriu as I turn to leave the room tells me that she will be crying, too. So be it. This is not a time for gentleness.

Carduc is at the front hearth and sees my anxiety.

"I am ready," I tell him. He does not try to calm me or feed me as Katha would. "Is our army assembling?" I call it an army but truly it is not, no trained soldiers, only tribespeople who must make themselves warriors, and like me, give reign to a malevolence they might not have known they even had. How many others of them will be surprised by what they discover they are capable of?

"My messengers say they have been assembling around the fort and in the village throughout the night."

"And our people–the shepherds and field workers?" I ask.

"Those who are coming have packed their wagons if they have one or loaded their horses if they do not. The ones who are staying behind are ready for instructions."

"Their instructions are simple," I respond. "They are to tend to the land and the animals."

"Some who are staying would have rather joined you," Carduc informs me. "There were not many volunteers to stay behind; I had to assign families. They would rather serve you in battle." He waits for my response, but I am still too upset over Grawnei to know what my answer should be. "They need to know that they serve you by staying here."

This is the Carduc my father relied on, and the one I must rely on. How else will I know what I am to do? His wisdom is reassuring though it stands in contrast to and reminds me of my own ignorance.

"Gather them," I tell him.

It is still dark but the activity in our yard and out among the huts of our property is the activity of mid-morning. My guards are already horsed and waiting, as are Leth and his men. Wagons are beginning to line up around the fields. Carduc leads the families of those who will stay behind to the yard, and I am there, mounted on a full-sized horse--not one of the mountain ponies–and in full ceremonial attire–cloak, bracelets, torque, helmet, sword–to greet them.

Without speaking, and with fervent Neidriu in mind, I ride my horse three times around this group, then come to a stop. "I have just prayed a blessing on you," I call into the dark dawn. "You will be protected as you protect this property. Your task here is not trivial. Not all who participate in a revolt carry swords to the battlefield. Those who stay behind do equally important work. When we return, Rome will have been chased from Britain. The time of tributes will be over. The land will be ours. You, field workers, you will tend the first crop in many years that will not go to pay Roman tribute. At the harvest, we will have much to celebrate.

"And you, herders, keep the cattle and the horses healthy. I may have to send for fresh horses. Who would provide them if you were not here? Now, beware, too. The Roman army in the west will soon hear about this insurrection. They may come through Iceni territory on their way to meet us. They may try to reclaim the land. You must join the others throughout the village who will stay behind, and hold the Romans back until our army can return to assist you. You may be the first Iceni that Paulinus faces. Be strong. Be brave. You will earn much honor."

I can see an inkling of pride in the nearest faces, but I see disappointment, too, and I am worrying as to what else I can say to encourage them, when from the center of the group comes a cheer. Now others join in.

Leth approaches with the horrible staff that is to inspire awful deeds from my people and remind them that I am capable of such awfulness, as well. The cheering grows louder.

Turning their horses, my guards position themselves in front of me, ready to lead our processional from the yard. The field workers and herders reluctantly clear a path; some will follow us into the village–some are already trotting ahead.

"To Camulodumnum!" I shout, and the guards start off. A pandemonium erupts. Shouting. Cheering. Clatter. Stomping. Barking. Behind me, the wagons have been aligned with a watchful eye to position. Somehow, an order has been decided on and enforced with those who are thought most important to me, nearest, and those who supposedly are least important, farther back. I want only to know that Katha, with my daughters, is close; that Carduc and Leth can come up on either side of me when I need their counsel and their company; that Leanan is behind Katha, bringing my chariot. Beyond that, everyone is of equal stature in my eyes, though the head herder and the head field-tender will believe they and their families deserve a close spot. And someone will say, "I provided the daughters with pups," and that person's family will move forward. Someone else will remember a request he fulfilled, and before they've left this yard, someone else will feel slighted, and unappreciated. "I work hard on this land, I show respect but I am treated coarsely." And there will be envy and resentment for the ones up front. And this, too, is the nature of my people. They are gentle; they are petty.

Garan meets us along the way and after greeting me, takes his place alongside Leth. I do not trust him, and am on alert, as I was yesterday, for an ambush he may have arranged. Leth and Carduc are suspicious, too, and I see them dispatch guards in every direction to search the woods. I summon Garan to me to see if I can determine by his countenance whether or not he will betray us. "Will you accompany us out of the village?" I ask. "I'd appreciate your companionship on the road to Camulodumnum."

"I'm honored to oblige." We speak with a feigned respect and a strained politeness.

I ask to hear his plan for the defense of the territory if that becomes necessary.

"Foremost," he begins as though he's been waiting to be asked, "I will begin training those under my command in the use of the sword. It has been a long time since anyone handled one. Some of the younger Iceni have never held one at all. An army is useless if it cannot handle its weapons."

This is clearly an insinuation. I have not taken the time to train my army. He is right. But there was no time, and no way. Should I have tried to train them right under Rome's nose? No. I could not. Instead of training, my army will have to rely on instincts and anger.

"We'll have contests," Garan continues, "with spears and slingshots. The games will prepare them for battle."

"And where will you station scouts?" I test him. "Your contests will amount to nothing if Paulinus arrives here surreptitiously. You cannot face him alone, Garan. You must be able to anticipate his arrival and get word to me."

"Of course," he says dryly, and I can sense that he believes he will not need me. Either Rome will not fight him because he will pledge his allegiance and join them when they arrive, and he is plotting that now as he rides within an arm's length of me, or he wants the glory of having faced a Roman army all to himself. And he would embrace utter defeat rather than share that glory.

He tells me his plan for scouts, but it doesn't matter. If Paulinus moves toward Icenia, I will know about it through my own scouts and will be back here before Garan can either join him or engage him. I will also need scouts here, I decide, ones who will watch Garan and keep me informed of his actions. He continues speaking, revealing a plan to build a wall around the village. Protected in the north and east by the sea, the wall would secure the western and southern borders. Though it will not stop Rome, it might delay them. "There is already enough work in the fields for those left behind," I argue. "How will they have time to build a wall?"

"I believe," he begins, "there are more efficient ways of farming. Fewer people can do the tasks that it takes many to do now if they work in an organized way. I am also devising a method of distributing food. Since there will be little of a market left, I have to ensure that everyone will be fed."

"Yes," I consider. "You will have to take from some families to give to others..."

"That is the only way," he interrupts.

"Yes. I am thinking, though, that we have only just been unburdened of the Roman tribute. For some, this will seem like a tribute of another sort. Is there some way of making payment for what you will take from them? Keep a record, at least. When I return, I'll offer something in exchange for the food they will have provided."

"This is not a tribute," Garan argues. "But if they want to call it that, let them. What matters is that everyone will be fed. That is my responsibility as their... leader."

If he meant to say "king" as I suspect he did, he caught himself just in time. He is right, again. Everyone must be fed; that is what is important. Still, I ask him to keep a record, tell him that I am confident in his leadership, and am satisfied with his plans. He wishes us success, and rejoins Leth.

As we near the village, my concerns about his ambush diminish, and my worries over whether a sufficient number of tribespeople will join me begin to wane, as well. We are joined by many who want to ride and run alongside us, who want to be part of the processional to the fort.

Raising my monstrous staff, I catch the scent of cedar oil, and though it has temporarily suspended the decay, it cannot completely disguise the stench of the flesh that had already rotted before Carduc soaked it. I must hold it to my side so that the northerly wind blows the odor away from me.

Soon, another scent reaches us–that of burned wood; its pungency is welcome, and I ride quicker toward it.

What comes into view is not what is left of the fort but the throngs of Iceni who surround it. Wherever I look, more people are coming. With difficulty, I move the processional through the crowds to the gate of the yard. The guards form a barrier for me, press the people back to provide a space for me to move in.

"Queen Boudicca."

"Boudicca."

"Iceni Queen."

"Boudicca."

"Avenger."

They reach for me.

"Boudicca."

My people. I am their queen. They have made me their queen, their hope. "The fort is burned," I shout, not having expected to give another speech. "The Romans, killed." I hoist Decianus's head, and listen to waves of cheers. "This Roman pig," I keep the staff high, "attacked my children, and conspired to take everything that was mine. He thought he would silence me, but see what has become of him." I thrust the head higher. More appreciation. "When all of Rome is driven back across the sea, everyone will know it was the Iceni who did it. Everywhere, stories will be told of us. They will speak of this day when we met at the ruined Roman fort. We will be remembered as warriors. All the children of the island will know of the great Iceni tribe who would not yield to Rome."

They are nearly frenzied with pride and anticipation. But it is not only their excitement that I want; I must have their rage, too.

"Now think, as I do, of the treatment Rome has meted out to you," I urge them. "Think of it clearly. The tributes paid. The children or husbands taken into slavery. The weapons they stole from us. The rapes," because maybe my daughters were not the only ones. "Forget nothing. Remember these abuses, and when you grow tired, think of them. When you have had enough battle and want to go home, think of what Rome did to you. And let your anger drive you. Now, on to Camulodumnum. And may the gods accompany us."

At this moment, someone from the crowd steps forward, showing me a wriggling hare she is holding.

"We heard of the hare you released at the fort," she shouts over the cheering. "If this one runs to the east as that one did, it is a good sign," she claims.

And if it runs to the west, I wonder.

I look to Carduc; he is as wary as I am. I'd rather march with no sign than risk a bad one. The woman sees my hesitation, and as though I had chastised her, bows her head and withdraws the creature. But her offer is already being repeated throughout the crowd. Refusal to face the challenge would indicate my doubt in our fate. Anxious eyes are on me. Handing off my staff, I dismount, take the hare, close it for a moment within my cloak so as to disorient it, and make this a true test, then face the direction of Camulodumnum.

Gods be with me.

I open my cloak and let the hare spring.

Gods, guide this creature.

It lands, and darts. To the east. Glad for its life. The crowd opens up a path for it, watches this sign make its escape.

Relieved cheers set this army in motion.

TWENTY-ONE

I am glad to be rid of him, having gone against Leth's suggestion and abandoned my staff at the ruins of the fort. Let Decianus remain there, the crows cawing over the last bit of his flesh. Let his skull serve as a warning to any Roman who crosses our territory. I could not bear to have him as companion any longer. Nor could Neidriu and Grawnei.

Carduc rides next to me now, and it is his thoughtful company that I want. His face shows little, not fear, not excitement, though I know that his impassive expression betrays the activity of his mind–considering contingencies, reviewing the signs–that he is busy at.

"Carduc," I disturb his reverie, "what do you think of Leth's hare? A good sign?"

As though he has been thinking of this question just as I asked it, he answers without taking time to consider. "One could read signs in everything, if that's what one wanted to do." His tone chastises me.

"But there *are* signs to be read in everything, aren't there?"

"Only if one knows how to read them."

I believe he is a Druid, not a formal one trained for the requisite twenty years, but he is a knower, a seer by birth or by careful observation of the world. Either way, he does know things. "Then how do you read the hare's flight, Carduc?"

"It ran to save itself."

I laugh, a short laugh, a quick exhalation more than a laugh, and yet the sensation of it– giddy release–rushes through my body.

I remember that he could make my father laugh unexpectedly, too, in the same way with these simply stated matters of fact in answer to some issue my father found profoundly complex. Carduc enjoys the sound of my lately unfamiliar laugh, and smiles at me, but I know that his intention is, as always, not to entertain but to instruct. "Indeed," I answer. "But then tell me, if the hare's choice of an easterly escape is not a sign, then what signs do you see?" I tilt my head back. "What, for example, are the skies saying?"

He casts his glance downward rather than upward. "You see the sky. What do you think it says?"

The old game he played with me when I was a girl: a question answered with a question. I am to discover that I already know the answer if only I will take the time to think about it. Looking upward, I respond, "I can tell you that the sky is clear; last night's was clear, also. But I can't say anything about the stars."

"What does a clear sky tell you?"

"Travel will be easy; there will be no rain. But that's all I see. Surely you see more."

"What more do you need to know than that there will be no rain today?" he asks.

"Is the time right for this action?" I ask.

"Do you think the sky holds that answer?"

"The night sky. You used to read it for my father. What do the stars say about our revolt?"

"What can they say?" he asks. He bobs with the pace of his horse. "If the stars say it is not a good time, could we go back and choose another time?"

"No."

"No, we cannot go back. The time is now whether the skies agree or not."

So, then, I reflect, we are bound by nothing but our own choices and our actions; there is freedom in that. But is it too bold, and are we so separate from the rest of the world? Isn't it blasphemous to believe that our own choices guide us and not the wishes of the gods who send us messages through the stars? I almost ask Carduc this, but he will only coax me into answering for myself, and this is not something I have understanding for–the gods and their wishes–and I would not tempt angering them by trying to comprehend that which is incomprehensible.

"Do you agree?" Carduc inquires.

There is only one answer now. "My father said a time would come. This must be the time." But if the stars were in a favorable alignment, wouldn't Carduc be happy to say so? Wouldn't we have agreed that Rome's deeds could not go answered, and then wouldn't he have offered to show me, tonight, how the stars agree, as well? But he offers to show me nothing. And so perhaps the stars do not agree. And yet this is the right time, the right action. I can let no sign dissuade me. Clever Carduc. Perhaps that is the lesson he wants me to learn. I can let no sign dissuade me.

We travel into the afternoon, then settle near a stream where we can rest for the night. There are those who do not want to rest, many who have waited thirteen years to pick up their swords again and who do not want to wait any longer. But a quicker pace would only exhaust them; we cannot be exhausted when we reach Camulodumnum.

As fires are started and meals prepared, Carduc and I visit the camps of my own field workers and herd tenders asking for consensus on two dozen of the tribe's swiftest riders. When it has been decided, after much disputation, those riders are sent to me.

They come expectantly to my camp, proud to have been chosen, curious about their assignment. Among them are several young women, wild-haired and with a look of playfulness about them, but confident, too, and sturdy. I can imagine them as girls, racing as I did, across fields, into the hills, a sweet friend just behind, friend, still, not lover, yet.

Tallas.

"You will ride ahead to Camulodumnum," I announce to this willing group. They pass glittering glances to one another. "You've been chosen for your speed and endurance, and so will be riding through the night. Between here and Camulodumnum is a guard house. You will kill the guards there, then ride on." I pause, watching their faces.

They force on themselves an impassivity, pretending that killing will come easily. "It is important that you arrive at Camulodumnum before dawn. I want you to do there what was done in Iceni territory–ambush the patrollers one at a time. Don't confront them as if you were an army. You are not an army. Take one man at a time. Kill him and drag him away. Make sure the body cannot be found. You are not to be seen by anyone who will carry word into the village of your presence. If you are discovered and the veterans organize a troop to attempt to capture you, ride south. Lead them away from the village and away from us. Kelvin..." I know one of the young men as the son of Lamerok, my head herder. "You will lead."

He bows his head respectfully and comes forward, trying to suppress his smile.

But he does not know yet what he is about to do. He knows of bravery in stories only; he will discover soon whether or not he possesses the quality, and whether it is bravery or fear he acts from when he kills. He will soon discover what violent acts he is capable of, and how those acts will separate him from the person he was before he knew what was inside him.

"If you are not chased," I continue, "then after you have killed them, wait in the woods. We will arrive that evening. You will join us then."

They are anxious to be off. But I hold them. "Your duty, do you understand, is to incite their fear. Let them know that something is in the woods, but do not let them know what it is. I want them to fret and guess. There is a statue," I remember, "built for Rome by Trinovante slaves, a statue they have boldly named Victory. It guards the village. Topple it if you can. Let them wake in the morning and tremble with its meaning. Let them know that something is coming for them."

There is determination in their faces. I hold them for one more instruction. "I want the Trinovantes to know only that a small band of Iceni is headed toward Camulodumnum. Kelvin, you will find a way to get that news to some of them. Instruct them to be ready to join that band. Now prepare what you will need and set out, and may the gods be with you."

Next, I assign two of my fieldhands–dependable and loyal men-
-to return to the village to observe and keep me informed of Garan's
activities. Though they surely realize that I am sending them as spies
and that I do not trust Garan, they restrain themselves from asking
the pointed question that might persuade me to articulate, out-
right, my distrust of him. What they cannot restrain, though, is their
disappointment.

"Then we are not to join you in battle?" one asks.

I regard them appreciatively. This is an important assignment, but
I do not want to abuse their loyalty. "I see that you are in a hurry to get
into battle. You may not feel that way once you see what fighting is. But
you want to be warriors, not messengers. Is that right? Return to Icenia.
Find Garan. Tell him I wanted to keep him informed of our position
and that that is why you have ridden back." Garan will feign appreciation but he is not so ignorant as to not suspect the real mission of these
men if I were to have them remain there. So, I will outwit him and give
these men the chance at battle that they want so desperately. "After
you have delivered your message, discretely choose two trustworthy
villagers and give them the task of observing. They will be responsible
for getting any critical news to me. And you will be responsible if they
don't. Choose well. I will see you in Camulodumnum."

After, more riders are sent west and south to inform the other
tribes and ask for their support.

As for a battle plan, it is simple, and with the help of the messengers, Carduc, Leth and I spread it throughout the camps.

"Kill every Roman you see," I tell the families. "Desecrate the temple to Claudius. We will greatly outnumber the veterans, but Rome
will put up a fight, no matter how futile. Be prepared. Know, too, that
many of the veterans have had their wives brought from Rome. Kill
them." There is no resistance to this command as Roman women are
ill regarded; there are no queens among them, no arms strong enough
to hold a sword. "Their children, too," I instruct and try not to show
my hesitancy, my own horror at this order. "No one is to be left alive.
We must show no mercy. They must see that we are willing to kill every
Roman in Britain if that is what it will take to rid ourselves of them."

My daughters are glad to see me that evening, but even with Neidriu there is still a certain reserve. She holds on to me but wants Katha and Leanan within her sight, too, and asks Katha for what she needs. Good. She is still afraid of me, but also seems to know that I cannot be wholly hers now, and she has already filled the space of my absence. Grawnei sits with her pup in her lap; her face expresses nothing, but her hand, which strokes him over and over, the fingers which twist his hairs and gently flip his ear demonstrate that there is still love in her, and need.

Later, the murmurings, the pungency of cooking meat, the smoky air, the fires bending along the curve of the stream extending beyond the range of my vision lull me, and I abandon my desire to worry over the coming days, and instead go willingly toward sleep, toward the place of dreams where sometimes, lately, Tallas comes to meet me.

When I wake, I don't remember whether I dreamed of him or not, but he is in my first thoughts, and I linger in the pre-dawn darkness under the warm blanket listening to the snorting and shuffling of the animals, the creak of the wagons as children arrange themselves within, the snapping of new fires, the soft, clear voices of early morning women. But as I dally, still within sleep's reach, there is no forgetting that by evening I will be outside Camulodumnum, and when I rise again tomorrow morning there will be no time for quiet moments; I will awaken with blood in my thoughts. But just a little longer here, while I am only Boudicca, under a warm blanket, not Queen of the Iceni whom I have made rebels. One moment to think of sweet things, to think of Tallas. We are riding together on his horse; I am holding him at his waist. My body embraces him—my knees are folded inside his, my breasts undulate against the active muscles of his back, his hair blows to my mouth, his shoulder lets my chin ride it. He turns for a quick kiss, missing my lips, gives the kiss to the wind.

But I still cannot recall him, not his face, not clearly. Here, my wrist to my mouth as though it is his neck. His neck. His smell. Tallas. I will find him; "I will find your face again."

The travelling is not difficult; we have the Roman-built roads to thank
for that, though they could not have imagined that their roads would
aid in bringing them their doom. I ride the chariot for a portion of the
journey so the girls can ride alongside me. The way is clear and direct.
The guard station that we pass is abandoned; I suspect the bodies of
the guards are in the woods being feasted on by any number of crea-
tures; good, let the animals sate themselves on Roman flesh. I assign
six of my own guards to the station, knowing that my people would like
to burn it down, needing to prevent them, as we are near enough now
that the smoke might alert the veterans of Camulodumnum. But the
sight of the derelict station stokes their confidence–there is cheering
and a surge forward as their desire to reach Camulodumnum becomes
more urgent. Leth joins me to say that they will be hard to hold back
once the village is in sight.

"I am tempted, too," I confess, "to ride in tonight." My body is
tense with readiness. But this is reckless; our strength would dissipate
quickly if we did not rest, and it is important, especially now at the
outset, that I do not give in to whim, do not let myself be swayed from
a plan without better reason than impatience.

That night I close my eyes, but they do not stay closed. I am alert
like an animal in the woods whose senses are sharpened to the danger
that is always near. Carduc sits up into the night; Katha joins him. She,
too, is restless; she has fed us, the oxen, our horses, and the girls' pups,
and has put the girls under a blanket in the wagon, and made sure I
was resting and not in need of anything. Now, temporarily without a
task, she brings a cup to Carduc and sits by him. Their voices are low,
and they watch the fire as they speak, then fall silent. When Katha rubs
her arms as though she is cold, Carduc moves nearer to her and takes
her into the blanket that is covering his shoulders, and they stare again
at the fire that lights their single form. Under the blanket, I imagine,
he rests his hand on her thigh. What satisfaction there must be for a
man in the fullness of his wife's flesh under his hand. After a short
while, Katha takes his hand from under the blanket, puts the back of

it to her mouth and holds it there, rubbing its roughness across her lips. He watches her as she does this, then whispers something, and she laughs, a hearty laugh that breaks into a chuckle. I could watch them all night, and I am disappointed when Katha gives Carduc back his hand, escapes from the blanket and walks toward me.

"Not sleeping yet?" she whispers.

"No."

"Go sit by the fire for a while," she suggests. "It will entrance you as it has me. I can't keep my eyes open."

"Sleep then," I say gently.

With my cloak, which is also my blanket, over my shoulders, I join Carduc. At first we are silent. The plan has been gone over, confidence expressed. There is not much more to say on it. But he does not stare blankly, entranced, as Katha was; instead he seems to study the flames, and I can't help but wonder what he sees there, what sign, even though he would deny such a thing. I look from him to the flames and try to find what it is, knowing that if I asked, he would only reply with "Tell me what *you* see." But I am no seer. The flames feed themselves on snapped branches–that is all I can discover there.

Katha is right; the fire quickly captivates me. When Carduc quietly says, "I knew of Tallas's plan for the rebellion," I can't pull my eyes away from the flames to look at him. I heard him clearly, and I understand, but my body responds with no surprise, no anger, and my eyes won't abandon the flames. "I learned of the plan the day before he undertook it. I did not tell your father."

Still, I let the fire hold me, even as I recall those days and see the meanings of what Carduc has said. My father, betrayed, not by me, as he believed, but by Carduc. Carduc, letting my father believe I was complicit with Tallas when all the while he knew I wasn't. Carduc, not joining Tallas. Carduc, knowing Tallas could not succeed.

"Your father would have stopped him," he explains, though I've asked for no justification for his behavior. "Tallas's preparations were hasty. I knew that he could not defeat that contingent of the Roman army; he knew it as well. But it was necessary for Rome to discover that opposition existed, that there were some who could see their intentions. It was a step, and that step had to be taken for us to arrive here tonight."

I am not thinking of Rome or of the step that had to be taken. I am thinking that one action–Carduc's informing my father–could have changed everything. Tallas could still be alive. My father, too. The marriage to Prasutagus might never have been demanded of me. Tallas could be alive. "Carduc..." is all I can utter aloud.

"The tribes will tell stories of Tallas," he continues, sorrowfully. "Just as they will tell stories of you. They will see that though years passed in between, one rebellion planted seeds of the other, and that one rebel picked up the work of the other. It is already happening. You live together in stories."

"I didn't want to live with him in a story, Carduc," I say, though the idea is not an unwelcome one. "I wanted to live with him in a marriage." I pause. "I can't even remember his face." And now I am tired. So tired. I rise and return to my mat on the ground and lie facing the sky.

Tallas, still alive. My father still alive. My heart plays with the impossible possibilities.

I sleep lightly and wake often. Each time I awaken, I see Carduc at the fire, once, rubbing his sword with a cloth; once, putting sticks on the fire; again, staring. The last time I awaken, I go to him. "It's time," I say.

Before we are ready to set out, Kelvin, and another from his group who rode ahead, come to me with news of their success. "We've been camped out there," he points to the east, "last night and the night before. We killed over thirty patrollers and toppled the Statue of Victory. Many of the citizens are running to the temple to make offerings and pray for protection," he ridicules them.

"Will the Trinovantes be ready to join us?" I ask.

"We couldn't risk going into the village to get word to them, but we marked the fallen statue with woad. We hoped they would recognize that as a sign from us."

"They will, and so will the veterans," I remind him. "Have they organized an army?"

"They're just old men," Kelvin scoffs.

"They're old soldiers," I remind him. "Trained and experienced."

He takes his reprimand with a bowed head, but I can see when he looks up again that I have not curbed any of his arrogance.

"Have they posted more guards?"

"Yes."

"How many?"

"I don't know. They were attempting to ring the village."

"Return to your position. Wait for my signal."

It takes some time to organize this sprawling army, for warriors to bid their families good-bye, leave children and wagons and come forward in some formation: horses and chariots up front, sling shooters behind, foot soldiers interspersed–many naked and blued, the way our stories tell us we have gone into battle before. Families, with their wagons and livestock organized at the rear, will remain on the outskirts of the village creating as much of a clamor as they can. It occurs to me as I watch these thousands ordering themselves that our mass may be a disadvantage. If we do outnumber the veterans as greatly as I suspect we will, then there will be not nearly enough Romans for each of my willing warriors to engage, and too many warriors on a battlefield may be as inefficient as too few. Leth has already thought of this, and when I voice my concern, he informs me that he has been arranging troops, assigning leaders in each one and determining a strategy for their deployment, but he advises me to let as many go as the battlefield--just outside the village--can accommodate. "Those held back would be insulted," he reminds me. "And now is not the time to insult or to dampen enthusiasm."

When we have achieved an order of sorts, we move again, and as we near the village, at Leth's direction, troops fan out on either side of me in a crossbow shape–more of a practiced formation than I expected of them.

Now we advance. Slowly, patiently. A Roman guard is in sight. Turn. I want him to turn. I want them to see us emerge from the woods. I want them to see us coming. Yes. Yes. Here we are. I signal a guard, and he blows vigorously through the conch. Shrieks erupt, and we charge.

My eyes never leave the Roman who was the first to turn and who is now trying to take in the number, the identity of the tribe that is descending on him. My sword is through him before he can make sense of us. Now they come. More Roman guards. From two directions. They are not much of a force; still, they will not fall without a fight.

Behind them, waiting at a short distance, are the veterans who have assembled themselves into an army. There seem to be more of them than I anticipated, but this could be one of their strategies–to arrange themselves to appear to be more than they are. We have no such strategy; we are as many as we appear to be. I cannot see beyond these Romans, and yet, I know we must outnumber them.

Their horsed soldiers lead a march toward us, their lines broken by the intervening trees; and yet the trunks seem not to compromise their wall but to fortify it, as if the trees were in alliance. Behind them with their shields edge to edge, the foot soldiers approach like a swarm of hard-shelled beetles. We are pelted with arrows, and for a moment I feel a swell of fear, not just mine but a collective fear, a stark realization of our actions, and of our enemy, and in this moment we falter, and I know the urge to turn and run is strong. But our slingers begin their assault, and shrieks join the arrows in piercing the air, and we rush forward away from that fear. I have another Roman in my sight. His short sword is no match for my long one as I come at him; I am splitting his arm open and dropping him from his horse before he is close enough even to prick me. Here, another one. My blade across his chest. Stubborn. He won't fall. I hit him again.

I have been counseled by Leth and Carduc to lead the charge and then remove myself to a safe spot–keep myself alive and uninjured for future battles. And now, already, I see Leth coming for me, signaling my guards nearby to circle my chariot and lead me out of the fighting. Then a quick, searing throb in my left arm. Instinctually, I go to grab it with my right hand and nearly let go of my sword. The Roman is already dead by the time I turn to him; Leth is shouting; the guards close around me, the reins are taken. I let them lead me away, appreciative of the fact that they must have always had me in their sights even while they fought, though I did not have them in mine. One guard rides ahead to find our wagon and Katha, then comes back and guides us there. My wound is not deep to the bone. But it bleeds excitedly.

Katha is ready for me. I am helped from my chariot, and expertly, the cut is tied off and cleaned. She determines that it requires sewing, and though I am able not to scream out at the pain, I cannot keep my stomach from lurching, and she has to stop more than once while I vomit.

My sword arm, too, I realize now that I have stopped moving it, is sore, not wounded but fatigued. So quickly. And many other inexperienced arms are tiring, too, I suspect. I survey the wide arc that the wagons make at the edge of the battlefield and glance back through the woods where others have set up temporary camp. There are already many wounded being tended. "So many injuries so soon?" I say.

Katha, intent on my wound, doesn't answer. She also doesn't ask about Carduc, and I wish I had something reassuring to tell her–that I saw him, and he was uninjured and fighting fiercely–but I lost track of him as soon as the battle began. I lost track of everyone, and I chide myself for that. This is something I must change; I must expand my awareness. Those around me should know that I see them, that I could assist if necessary. To be confident, we need to know we can depend on one another.

Despite Katha's insistence, I won't rest. I need to be seen–up and strong, not resting this early in the battle.

Now that the blood is cleaned up and the wound closed, Leanan brings my daughters. Neidriu rushes at me, but Leanan holds her back. "Careful, your mother's been hurt," she explains.

"But not badly, little one," I assure her. Katha smiles at me, a bit sadly perhaps–I am no longer her "little one." Neidriu hugs me gently. And even Grawnei, after some hesitation, pushes up against me in an awkward embrace.

"My sword needs cleaning, Grawnei," I tell her. "Will you wipe the blade for me?"

Her eyes spark–just a flash, then it is gone, but I did see it. "Neidriu is 'little one.' What shall we call you? Wipe it good. Remember, this was the sword of a king. Do you remember, Grawnei, when I told you of your grandfather? Do you remember that I told you he gave me his sword? This sword will be yours one day. Just as my father passed it down to me, I will pass it to you, my oldest daughter. Clean it thoroughly. Wipe all the Roman blood away. Be careful," I remind her, "the blade is sharp on both sides." She works assiduously; Neidriu stands alongside, deferentially yielding this honor to her older sister. I drink a cup of mead, eat something of a stew that Katha has prepared and feel my strength reviving.

———

When Grawnei offers me the sword, I examine it, though only as a gesture to her hard work–a quick wiping would have satisfied me. "You have done a thorough job," I tell her, and she drops her eyes to hide her pleasure.

"Don't go," Neidriu blurts, seeing that I am preparing to return to battle. Then, like her sister, she averts her eyes, ashamed, I think because she was not brave enough to resist calling out her desire.

"You know I must go back. But you'll see me again soon."

She sniffles, then lifts her chin as a way of composing herself.

Katha eyes me with disapproval. "You're not strong enough."

I know that. But I can't sit back here, either. I turn to Leanan. "Would you bring the chariot?"

She does and offers to accompany me. "The Trinovantes have been joining. My sons..." she reminds me hopefully. "Perhaps they are there somewhere."

I direct Leanan to run the chariot, away from the engagement but close enough for me to be seen, close enough for the Romans to see that I am not stopped, close enough for my people to see that I am still with them. I ride with my sword held up in the air, though my arm quivers with the strain. From this periphery, I can see that there are so many of us, and each one wants so badly to make a killing that we are

160

breaking their ranks and ours, forcing them to engage us individually. And we are pushing them back toward the village; some of the fighting is already spilling into the alleys between the huts. I can see the Romans yielding ground. I can see their defeat.

It is not much longer before those Romans who are left know what I know–that their death is imminent, and now their soldierly courage abandons them, and they begin to run for the presumed safety of the temple.

"Claudius will not protect you," I shout. "Claudius will not protect you." Now I rejoin our army, and those who hear my shout pick up the chant.

"Claudius will not protect you."

Let them pray to their man-god. Let them quaver when he does not reply.

By nightfall, the floors of Claudius's temple are slippery with blood. The bodies of old men, soldiers, women, children sprawl on the cold floor–sacrifices to their emperor-god.

Exultant, we spend the night celebrating. Our losses are not many, and the bodies of those who were killed are buried or burned by their families. Stories of the battle are told and exaggerated. I stay by my own fire, but in the camps nearest to me–those of my field hands and herders–loud tales are told of the number of Romans they killed; if each warrior killed as many Romans as they say they did, we would have been wildly outnumbered. Yet, some of the men insist, Kelvin for one, arguing for the right to the champion's portion of the meal–the first and largest serving offered to the bravest warrior. One of his fellows defends his claim. "I saw him kill at least one hundred men," he says, giving up his own claim to honor for the chance to be invited by the champion to sit at his right side.

"My first," Kelvin calls him proudly. And if Kelvin is determined champion, as seems likely now, that is the appellation this boy will be called by—"Kelvin's first."

The children of these camps want to reenact the scenes of battle, but they bicker over their roles, no one wanting to play the despised and disgraced Romans. Grawnei and Neidriu look on, entertained by the quarreling, too timid to join in. Roasted pig is plentiful, as are mead and wine. And I am both hungry and thirsty. Leth and Carduc travel among the camps spreading my praise, assuring the people of my health. And after the eating, the singing begins. My name floats to me from various voices, in various tones: Queen of the Iceni; Brave Queen; Brave Boudicca; Killer Mother; Mother's Vengeance. I hear my daughters' names, as well. And: Claudius; Catus Decianus; Prasutagus. But I do not hear "Tallas." No one sings of Tallas. Boudicca and Tallas. Where are the songs Carduc promised? Where are the stories?

Later, just as sleep is forcing itself on me, Leth returns, having enjoyed the hospitality of several camps. He informs me that many of the Trinovantes have joined us, though they keep their camps separate. He tells me, too, of looting in the village, which I expected. "Some see it as payment," he explains.

"They know when they joined me that I could not pay them," I say with some disappointment.

"Still, some see payment as their right, and this looting is their payment. I think it is not payment from you they want, but payment from Rome."

"Then let them take what they can from the ruins."

"But," Leth worries, "if one group raids, and another group does not... If one group takes, while others take nothing..."

"There will be resentment," I finish his thought.

"And divisiveness," he adds.

"Yes. Then organize a looting party from each camp," I recommend. "Send guards to keep order. Have weapons collected first, and any uninjured horses. Then livestock, and wine, and sacks of grain, but not more than can be traveled with. When those useful items have been gathered, tell them they may claim any coins or jewelry that they find. But hoarders will be treated as thieves, let them know that, and killed or sent to live outside the tribe." I consider, "They deserve to take from Rome after all that has been taken from them, and I did encourage them to keep Rome's abuses prominently in their memories, but they must not let greed guide them. That is the Roman way, not ours. Remind them. And," I add, "inform them that we will break camp late tomorrow."

"So soon?" Leth asks.

His concern surprises me. "It won't be long before Paulinus hears of this attack," I remind him. "Word always finds a way to travel. By now some of those who escaped from Camulodumnum are carrying the news west." I am so sure of it that I can almost feel Paulinus's eyes on me; the old and constant sensation of being watched is not put to rest by purging Rome from our territory. "Are guards posted around the village and in the woods?" I ask, suspecting a presence that can't be there.

"Some."

"Assign more."

"I will." And then respectfully, he asks, "May I offer my opinion?"

"Of course. I value your wisdom and want you always to speak freely with me."

He nods appreciatively. "Two weeks ago these people were paying tributes and having their families taken away from them to cover debts. We were restricted from assembling. Now, they've defeated Rome. Twice already. They feel victorious, and it is important that you let them celebrate that. And rest. They've traveled hard and fought well. Give them a day to savor their victory. If you don't, the victories will quickly become hollow for them, and their service to you, a duty, but not an honor. And," he adds, "forgive me, but it is our way to celebrate, to feast."

I put up my hand to stop him, impatient with myself, not him, for forgetting the significance of this feast. "Yes, they should feast. They should celebrate. It is our way, isn't it? Or was. To enjoy a victory, a good harvest, good fortune with celebration. But we have not defeated Rome yet," I warn him. "What we have faced is not the true Rome."

"No," Leth agrees, "but we fight not only to defeat Rome but to regain our right to be Iceni or to be Trinovante. To remember how."

I smile. "They are remembering, aren't they? It is as though they are awakening from a long slumber. Let them celebrate. But only for another day. Then we move. Early."

Leth smiles.

"It is a victory, isn't it?" I ask.

"It is."

"Thank you, Leth."

The full exhaustion of the day settles on me again, and I must admit, I am glad for another day of rest. I lie down on the mats, under the canopy that Katha has set up for me. Tonight my daughters join me, one on either side, their pups in their nests beside them. The sounds of celebration are still distinct, though the songs, now, have taken on a melancholy quality. But this is the way of celebration; it must yield to remembering, and remembering often brings sadness.

The sky is dark, and where it meets the earth, I cannot tell. Those glimmering points in the distance–are they fires or stars? Fires or stars? Either one, they dance. Good signs. They must be good signs.

In the morning I am sore. Leth was right to have us wait another day. My arm, where the wound is, is heavy, my sword arm and legs are stiff. Even my neck will not turn its full range. I get up like an old woman, slowly, gracelessly, and straighten my resistant back a little at a time. Katha sees me struggle and suggests a walk "to get the body used to moving again." It does help, eventually, though at first it is only more discomfort.

Leanan was up early, Katha tells me, wondering about her boys. "I told her to take a horse and go look in the camps. Maybe they're with some of the Trinovantes. It will be difficult for her to leave tomorrow if she hasn't found them by then," Katha laments.

"Yes. I suppose she can stay behind to look for them if she likes, though it's not probable the boys are still in the village."

"They could be hiding," Katha suggests, hopefully. So like a mother in her concern for these boys; she is no less a mother because she did not have children of her own.

"I can spare a few guards to stay back with her for a day or more, if that is what she wants."

"I'll tell her," Katha offers, "but I don't think she'll stay."

"She'll find them," I offer. "Others have been found."

Katha agrees, though not with any enthusiasm.

Carduc is busy sharpening swords with his stone. He glances at me, then away, as if ashamed. I want to say something to him, but there is nothing to be said. That I forgive; I don't know if I do. That his silence about Tallas's rebellion was right; but how could betraying my father be right? That I don't want enmity between us? I don't, and yet, can I trust him now? If he betrayed my father, will he betray me? But I don't believe that. He won't betray me. I know that better than I know anything. Just now, as I look at him, I know that. He looks again. I hold his gaze. Let that tell him something–that I still need him. That he must stay near. That I blame him. That I don't. That there are too many words but none can serve me now. Impotent words. Imprecise words.

Words. I am thinking a dangerous thought. A thought I will never say aloud. Words. I am thinking that it is all only words. That Rome is only words. A story. One I can choose to disbelieve. Paulinus will come soon, but can his army be any greater than mine? Do we fear him because he is so formidable or because we have been taught to fear him? He is daring, yes, slaughtering the Druids, but they were unarmed. Isn't that cowardice? Rome has strength, yes, but that strength has been aggrandized by stories we have been told of them, and stories we have told ourselves. Stories. Words: Empire; Caesar; Power. Maybe only words.

Oh, but there are other words, too, I remind myself. Tribute; Slavery; Rape. Rome taught us these, and these aren't impotent. And if these are Roman words, what are our words? There is only one for us: Iceni. And one for the Trinovantes: Trinovante. And those words must stand against all of theirs.

Then it is critical that Grawnei speak, isn't it? And it is clear to me why her silence unsettles me so. It *is* a sign. Let Carduc say there are no signs; there are, and this is one. Our words–our word–overcome by their words. Grawnei must reverse the sign and overcome their words with ours. She must speak and give our word potency.

Last night's celebrating has done both she and Neidriu some good. They have remembered old friendships, and are letting some of the children who live on our land play with the pups. But as I approach, I notice a pall over the group.

"Mother." Neidriu passes her pup from her lap to her friend and stands up to hug me.

"Are you playing?" I ask her. "You are all so quiet."

Neidriu hesitates, then looks down at the ground, anticipating my displeasure. "It was a contest. To be quiet like Grawnei. I'm sorry, Mama."

All our children, silenced, teaching themselves silence. Rome will have done its work well if our own children become practitioners and teachers of Rome's will. "Yes, you should be sorry. That's not a game to play. Now, go see Katha. Take your pup." The two friends glance up at me, their eyes full of awe. What stories have they heard of me? What exaggerations? Whatever the stories are, they know the time is right for them to scurry away, and they do so, back to their camps.

"Grawnei, stand." There is nowhere to walk where I could find the solitude for us that I want now. I guide her toward our fire, and seeing us approach, Katha, who is already soothing Neidriu there, takes her to the wagon. "Silence is not a game to play, Grawnei." It isn't her fault. She wants to tell me that she did not encourage the contest. But yes, she did. "Whether you asked them to join you in your silence or not, you encourage them. Neidriu watches everything you do and imitates it, you know that. I do not want her to go quiet, too. Do you understand?"

She shows me sad eyes.

"You're close, Grawnei. I can see it, so close to speaking. Let the words come out. You want to tell me. What is it?"

Gently, I entreat her, "Tell me what happened in your room that day. Tell me now, and never tell another person. Whisper it. Whisper it so quietly that I don't even hear it. And then never say those words again. Throw *those* words away from you. But not all words, Grawnei."

She swallows hard and blinks; she is thinking of that day, seeing it, but then quickly she forces her face to go blank again. "When you were little, Grawnei, I used to whisper to you. Do you remember? I whispered a name. Do you know it? Tallas. Tallas is that name." She is holding herself rigidly, straining for impassivity. "He was your father, Grawnei. You did not know him but he was your father. And I loved him. But he was killed. Murdered by Rome. You were growing in me when they killed him. You were there in me when I watched them kill him. They killed him because he was brave. They were afraid of him, Grawnei. He was not afraid of them; they were afraid of him. Afraid because he spoke against Rome; he fought against them. He would not let them silence him. Do you hear me? He would not be silenced. Now think, Grawnei, you have a responsibility as his daughter. A responsibility to speak, to make him proud. Come, Grawnei, a word. Just a word."

Nothing.

"The tribe needs your voice."

She stares into the fire; her forehead furrows, and I wait. A word, just a word.

"Grawnei."

But she will not speak. If there was a moment when she might have, it has passed. As I have before, I take her roughly by the shoulders. "This is willfulness, daughter. Sheer willfulness. Speak. Speak, Grawnei. Obey me." She refuses, and now, I slap her, once across the cheek. "Speak." She tries to blink away the tears, but they fall. "I don't want tears. I want an answer." The crack of my hand on her face has drawn Carduc's, Katha's and Neidriu's concerned attention. "Go," I command her. And to Katha, "Take her. She is a stubborn child. A selfish child who cares nothing about her family or her tribe."

Katha clucks and rescues Grawnei into the harbor of her arms.

I take a horse, intending to ride off away from the silence, away from the terrible meaning that I can't help giving it. There are too many people, too many wagons, and this feeds my agitation. Finally, I am able to take the horse to a trot, and I direct it along the western side of the battlesite. Many of the bodies of the Roman soldiers have been picked naked. Yes, leave them naked.

I ride into the village, two Iceni women exit, smiling and carrying sacks, from a house. When they see me, they hurry away, back toward their camps with their booty. My warnings clearly haven't deterred hoarding. Further on, I discover a group of Roman women being guarded by three young Iceni men.

"Queen Boudicca," one of these young guards addresses me, "we found them hiding in their homes."

I regard him and then these women. "My orders were clear," I say coldly. "No captives."

"Yes ma'am," he stammers. "Yes, but we found them today, just a short while ago." He looks at me hoping for understanding. "It was after the battle."

"And so because they did not participate in the battle, because these women were found, cowering probably, after the killing had been done, you young men could not murder them? I want no captives," I repeat.

The youth nods.

"Strip them," I decide, a violence swelling in me. "Did they expect mercy?" I dismount and go to one of the women; she is soft-armed, soft-faced. "Do you know what your men do to Iceni children?" I ask.

She whimpers.

"This." I tear her tunic from her shoulder. She covers her breasts. False modesty, I decide taking my dagger from my belt. Quickly, I pull it across her throat. She drops. "Kill them," I demand of the other seven, calling over their cries. But their deaths are not enough. What do I want from them? Their fear. Their suffering. That which Rome has demanded of us. Their voices. Yes, their voices in this world and the next. I ride back to our camp, order needle and thread from a perplexed Katha and return purposefully to the women whose throats now have been slit.

"Sew their mouths," I command and see an exchange of worried looks among the guards. "Sew their mouths shut," I shout and begin on my woman. Through her upper lip–thick flesh still responding with blood–down through the lower, crossing her mouth with monstrous stitches.

When it is done, I am still not satisfied.

"I want them hung," I tell the frightened young men. "Their bodies run through with stakes, or posts. This way." I indicate a lengthwise impaling, moving my hand from my neck to my belly, slowing it there, sliding it down further, watching the faces of the men, as my hand stops at the point which will be the place of entry. Their eyes widen. "And plant them where the statue of Victory stood. They will greet anyone who comes to Camulodumnum."

—

A day later, when we ride out of Camuldomunum, back through the village and toward the road that will lead us to Verulamum, my daughters stare back at the silenced women. Their mother's work. Grawnei glances at me, then away.

TWENTY-TWO

Bloody needle. It jerks me awake.

And still Grawnei will not speak.

All there is is killing. I look ahead, and there is killing. And beyond the killing, I can't see. What amount of blood, what number of bodies will show me the time beyond the killing?

Here, I close my eyes, and the needle points at me again. My lips. It wants my lips. Then Grawnei's. Now, my hand holds the needle, and it wants Grawnei. Stitches across her lips. Her mouth sewn shut. And mine sewn, too, by me.

And silence.

Silence.

TWENTY-THREE

Verulamum offers no more resistance than Camulodumnum did. Without my urging, women are impaled, staked at the entrance to the city, their mouths stitched in an ecstasy of brutality. Still, it doesn't satisfy me. I could order a hill of heads to be assembled, a mound of legs. I could cleave chests open and set torches in the cavities, so insatiable am I for violence during the battle. My cruelty reminds me of their cruelty; my mercilessness, of their mercilessness. Nothing I do to Rome mitigates what they have done to us. Nothing I take from them replaces what they have taken. Instead, the more I kill, the more abused I feel, the worse my acts, the sharper my memories of abuse become. And yet, I feel that somehow, I must be more barbarous than they, more ruthless to truly overcome them.

My army feels it too—victory, yes, and they celebrate again. Eat and drink gluttonously. Loot, viciously. Like my vengeance, their avarice cannot be sated. They want all that Rome had; I cannot unteach them the lessons of greed that they have learned so well. Their unruliness threatens the loose order that holds us together. Dobunni and Coritani who have joined us from the west. Atrebate and Cantiaci from the south. United. United with the Iceni in their rapacity, united in their suspicions that one or all of the other tribes has taken a larger share of the booty. United in their distrust of one another.

Leth sends more guards to oversee the looting parties.

"Find someone to punish," I tell him. "Make an example." Then I change my mind. The tribe of the one singled out will call me unfair, prejudiced against them. I can't risk losing any support. "Just try to keep them from fighting with one another," I instruct instead.

After the battle, my violence wanes. I don't want to look back at the mutilated women we've left standing like hideous scarecrows over our crop of bloodied Romans; they make me fear myself. Why do I punish the women? Worse, why do I want now, afterward, to stop punishing them? Why am I sorry for my deeds?

I don't want to see the needle when I close my eyes, or imagine the force of the stake thrusting itself into those women, into me, or see the hill of limbs that tempted me while I was raging. I want silence. Silence of my voice and of my mind. I want what I have stopped asking Grawnei to surrender. I want to share with no one the further brutality I longed to afflict. I want to order nothing, inquire about nothing, arrange nothing. I want the words and the gory images that the words command to seep from my mind and my grasp. I want to remove myself the way Grawnei has removed herself. Be elsewhere. Not here. I want to see beyond the blood. And silence, I think, is the only transport. In silence, I am not "Bloody Boudicca." In silence, there was a time before this. I want silence to lead me to that time, to rinse the blood from my thoughts.

Yes, there was a time when I gave up the contests with the boys, with Tallas–the running, the dagger throwing, the fishing, the fighting. I fought them with my hands to prove my strength. Then was I always violent? But I gave it up. Yes. I gave it up to learn from Katha. Weaving and dyeing. And cooking. "So now you want to be a girl and not a boy," she teased me.

"A woman," I corrected her.

"Ah," she nodded. "Nothing less than a woman."

"Show me."

"Show you what?"

"How to be a woman."

"What is it to be a woman?" she asked me.

"What you do."

"What do I do?" she asked.

"You're acting like Carduc," I accused her, impatiently, "with all your questions."

She laughed. "I am, aren't I? I'll teach you to weave and to cook," she said, her air of busyness returning. "Tonight you'll season the meat. You'll mix the vinegar and the herbs. You'll watch the meat over the fire. But that won't make you a woman."

"No?" I asked with disappointment.

"Are you strong?" she asked. Now she was impatient. "And brave?"

"Yes."

"Then you are already a woman," she concluded, "and now you'll be a woman who can cook and weave. Get me those jars."

She taught me to be brave and gentle. I was gentle once. Not now. But once. Not so long ago.

———

In the morning, messengers bring the news. Paulinus is moving east.

"Eat and rest," I direct the messengers. "Don't spread the news of Paulinus's movement any farther, just now." They exchange a look, and I know by it that I am not the first to receive the announcement; they have spread it already. Then there'll be a commotion soon, but I want a short time with the knowledge, a short time to feel it before planning for it, a short time to hear in my head all that it brings up. But first, the messenger continues.

"There's more," I'm told. "Two small units of the army in the south are coming north. They may mean to intercept us and are only a day away."

"Yes. You've done well. Now eat and rest." And leave me to my thoughts.

Paulinus. The Roman army. The army without which Rome would not be Rome. Moving toward us in quick soldier-step. And then it will be over. The killing over. And I will be able to see an end to the blood, though first, there will be more of it. Roman blood. Iceni blood.

He is coming, and here is my virulence again. I will carry his head on a staff. "Here is the great Paulinus who called himself governor. And the great Roman army." A head will bounce on each Iceni harness. "Look at the great Roman army." And when we return home, a head will mark each hut so that anyone who comes to our territory will know that here are the great Iceni who slaughtered the Roman army.

And then it will be over. Truly over. And "Rome" will only be a word we use in stories. My daughters' children will only know "Rome" as a word.

Or.

Or "Iceni" will only by a word, a word the Romans despise enough to forget. A word they will not speak. No stories. No "Iceni." No "Boudicca." No "Tallas and Boudicca." Only "Rome." And then it will be over.

—

My army is not ready to be moved yet. Their looting is not completed, and they still need rest. But there are those who can be called on, those who take the Roman gold but do not need it to entice them to a fight. Leth organizes two thousand of them, though our scouts tell us that the Roman units in the south are no more than a few hundred men.

I leave Leth behind to prepare the army to travel, and Carduc, too, though he insists that it is unwise of me to travel without Leth or him.

"I have guards," I tell him. "I need you and Leth here." And I do not want him with me. I am not ready to forgive him. I owe it to my father, I believe, to Tallas, too, to show Carduc some disfavor, at least. Petty thoughts at so momentous a time. And soon I regret them, and miss his counsel.

—

Once it is over, I can see my mistakes so clearly. Our reports were right, and there were fewer than a thousand Romans in the army of Petillius Cerialis. The second troop, under Posthumus, lost courage and never joined Cerialis. Our advantage, however, was diminished by the narrow-ness of the road that I chose as a battlesite. I should have met Cerialis in the woods, or named an open area and sent word to him to find me there. Instead, I waited on the road, and surprised him, though some of that surprise, I realize now, was probably for the incompetence of my strategy. We rushed at them, but were restricted on the crowded road-way from effectively swinging our long swords. The Romans pushed forward, jabbing their short swords, chopping through our front line and several lines behind that. Then covertly, the Roman army divided itself, and before we knew what was done, half was at our backs, forcing us to face them in two directions. In time, this was their undoing. But at first, our warriors at the rear were caught unawares, and we suffered losses. Finally, to save ourselves, we spilled from the road into the bor-dering woods, and there we gained the advantage where the Romans were forced, as happened in Camulodumnum, to break from their lines and face us individually. Those we didn't kill, fled.

But we left Iceni bodies behind, too, many more than would have been left if I had chosen a better site or thought before Rome did of dividing the army and coming up behind them before they came up on us. I tell it to Leth and to Carduc.

"It is a victory," Leth encourages me.

But it is not celebrated.

Later, as I sit alone by the fire, I hear hushed voices and sad songs, and surely the facts of my ineptitude are recounted. And this night, I think I hear Tallas's name linked with mine. Tallas and Boudicca. Tallas and Boudicca. The same error. He chose a narrow embankment; she chose a narrow embankment. Tallas and Boudicca. But whether this is said or just imagined by me, I can't be sure.

Now the doubt in myself that has always accompanied me–perhaps my insatiable violence is a way of attempting to mask it–runs rampant, and I can't make a decision. Paulinus is less than two weeks away. We could rest, choose a position and wait for him. I could send troops to meet him, sacrifice those tribespeople in an attempt to diminish his numbers somewhat and to tire him.

Yes.

Or we could move onto Londinium. I have promised Londinium, the trading center, to my army, and the goods there would be abundant enough to satisfy everyone. One more Roman village before we face Paulinus. One more victory to send us confidently to Paulinus.

Yes.

But to cut his numbers down would be wise. But the sacrifice, the death. And our numbers would be cut, too. I don't want more Iceni death on my hands. Or more Catuvellauni. Or Dobunni.

Then it will be Londinium.

Carduc joins me at the fire, though I have asked to be left alone. At first, he says nothing. And I will not, either. I will not show him my vacillation, or show my concern for what is said in the camps tonight about Boudicca who nearly led her troops to slaughter.

But Carduc has power over me, and before long I am thinking aloud, "Perhaps it is time for Leth to lead."

"The tribes follow you," he states simply.

"They would follow Leth."

"Yes."

"Women do not lead the Romans into battle. Perhaps Rome is right in that. Perhaps our people would prefer a man's leadership."

"When our people follow," Carduc instructs me, "they do not follow a man or a woman. They follow a leader."

"They doubt my ability."

"They doubt or you doubt?" he asks.

"Both," I admit.

"So, you would take this lesson from Rome and let yourself believe that a woman, because she is a woman, cannot lead."

I don't answer.

"And you've taken a lesson from Tallas, as well," he says, surprising me with the mention of Tallas's name when he must know that in my mind he has lost his right to speak of Tallas or my father. "But what you've learned from Tallas was never true. I've watched the rage that overcomes you. And I understand it. Rome has given you good reason for rage. But I think, too, that the rage is your way of battling a weakness you perceive in yourself. The rage gives you strength, determination. Strength and determination that you believe you don't have." He pauses. "Do you remember Tallas's revolt?"

Yes, and I made the same mistake he did. Is that what Carduc wants me to admit?

"And you remember why he never told you of his plan," he continues without waiting for my answer. "Why didn't he tell you?"

"Why do you want me to remember this, Carduc? You are cruel. Tallas didn't tell me because he couldn't trust me. Unlike you, I would have told my father and stopped Tallas. I still wish he could have been stopped. After all Rome has done to us, all the evil that I now know they are capable of, I still would have prevented him from having his rebellion."

"You loved him," he says. "It's natural for you to have wanted more time with him. And he loved you. Why then have you never considered the possibility that the reason he didn't tell you was that he loved you and trusted you? Trusted you so much that he was sure if he told you, you would join him. And he loved you too much to let that happen."

I shake my head. "I wouldn't have joined him. I would have stopped him."

"Perhaps. Perhaps not."

I will not consider it. It is not true. But... it is tempting. But no. "Carduc, you can't know that Tallas felt that way. Did he tell you that? Did you speak to him about me?"

"Why do you resist believing? He had faith in you. Your father had faith in you, or he wouldn't have entrusted you with his sword. You disappoint them both by so easily giving up faith in yourself."

After a few moments of silence, he leaves me to think about what he has said. Can it be true? Did Tallas trust me? Did you, Tallas? But I would have stopped you; I know I would have stopped you. And what difference does it make now when I can't even see your face? What does it change? Nothing. I still can't find your face.

All night by the fire, I still can't find your face.

TWENTY-FOUR

Two days from Londinium, and though I have the army sleeping in units, warriors up front and in the rear, families in between in case of ambush on the road, I want to break my own command and sleep back with my daughters tonight.

Poor Neidriu. In these last days of battle and travel, she has given herself up to Leanan and Katha, and her shame in what she thinks is her disloyalty to me is exhibited in her attempt to refuse to look at them while I am with her. Grawnei–I don't know what she feels, and I look at her and think we'll never know each other again.

Neidriu coaxes her pup into a demonstration of a trick for me. She tickles its ear with a twig, and the pup responds by scratching at the ear with a hind leg.

I laugh. "That's quite a trick. Does yours do a trick, too, Grawnei?"

"Hers does it," Neidriu assures me.

"Show me," I ask Grawnei. But Neidriu–now acting as the older sister, protecting the more fragile, sparing Grawnei from the wrath which Neidriu is clearly afraid will follow when her sister receives my request as though she is deaf as well as mute–takes her twig, and repeats on Grawnei's pup what she did to hers. The pup scratches.

I lie down with them. As much as it frustrates me, Grawnei's silence also seduces me, and I, too, could happily lie here with them and say nothing. Feel their bodies against mine, and say nothing. But it would frighten them, wouldn't it, their mother's silence? Frighten them as much as the daughter's silence frightens the mother.

"Shall I tell you a story?" I will tell stories so that in their memories will be a mother who tells stories and not only a mother who kills and makes monsters out of corpses.

"Yes."

I kiss Neidriu on the head. Let Grawnei want a kiss, too. Let her ask me for it. But no, she won't. I kiss her, too.

I tell them of Belinus and Brennius and their sacking of Rome before Rome even knew of Britain. "Once there were two brothers..."

"Like two sisters," Neidriu adds. "Like us."

I tell them of Cassivelannus who refused Julius Caesar when he demanded tribute and obedience from Britain, who sent Caesar back to Rome twice in defeat. I tell them of the celebration after the second victory, and of a fatal argument after the celebration between a nephew of Cassivelannus and the nephew of a duke of Britain. "When Cassivelannus's nephew was killed he ordered the duke's nephew to be brought to him, but the duke, Androgeus, suspecting that Casivelannus would punish his nephew, refused, and sent his nephew away. Now Androgeus began to fear that Cassivelannus would retaliate against him, so he sent a message to Caesar begging for his return and seeking his protection." I tell them how Cassivellannus, caught by surprise by Caesar's return and disheartened by the number who now joined with Androgeus and Caesar–many of whom had been recently celebrating Caesar's defeat–surrendered and was forced to agree to the payment of tribute.

I tell them, too, of Guiderius, Androgeus's grandson who became king and refused, unlike his grandfather, to honor Rome. And I tell them of Vercingetorix.

"Father didn't want us to talk of him," Neidriu remembers.

I don't tell them that their father was not brave. Kind, but not brave. I say," Your father would want you to know now." I tell them of Caratacus and of a "boy named Tallas." Grawnei glances at me, recognizing the name. Her father. "A young boy, handsome and brave with eyes that changed from blue to green."

"Grawnei's eyes change," Neidriu notes.

"Yes they do, don't they? Then she must be as brave as he was. Those eyes are only given to the bravest."

Before I sleep, I promise them each, in a whisper, that Rome will never touch them again. This is a vow that will not be broken. In the morning, I remind Carduc of the herbs I had asked him to collect when we first set out for Camulodumnum.

"Katha has the sack. The powder should be added to milk or mead."

I only look at him; I do not nod. To nod would be to understand, and how can I understand? To nod would be to calmly accept the plan, even to set it in motion. To agree that I will shake this sack over their cups of milk, have them drink it and then watch them die. To nod is to say that I can kill them; if that is the only way to protect them, I can kill them.

Carduc reaches a hand to me. Veiny blue under the weathered skin. I watch my hand go to his, watch his close around mine, feel the strength, the courage he offers me. The fellowship. "Carduc..." He squeezes my hand, and shakes his head as though to tell me that some things should not be given words; this is one of those things.

Paulinus fast-marches his army. My scouts report that he is only a half-day outside of Londinium. He waits for us there. I send the news through the camps. Paulinus awaits us in Londinium. Paulinus awaits us in Londinium.

That day we travel steadily, solemnly, with Paulinus and his army no longer a distant phantom but our near future. At night we sleep in shifts and keep a close eye on the road toward Londinium.

Tallas's face still does not come to me–a glimmer of it, a hint, enough to make me think I will have him again, enough to want him, but then the hint is gone. And now, with Paulinus so near, I try once more to see past Rome, past this imminent battle to our future and our home. I can see my daughters with their pups, but that is yesterday's memory–the pups scratch their ears. I can see Carduc at his small kiln; that is a memory, too. So, I will bring the memories into the future, place them there in the time after Paulinus, after Rome, after this last battle. Pleasant memories only, and our future, then, will be like our past except that there will be no Romans, and everything will be different.

He does not ambush us in the night, as I thought he might. But in the morning I discover that another kind of ambush has taken place--stealthy decampments during the night, sudden dartings of Iceni into the darkness. I swear shame on these whose courage failed them--promise that they will not walk among us in the village when the fighting is over, banish them beyond our territory, name them criminals. I must swear consequences or more will run tonight.

We travel again at a constant pace and with sober thoughts. How many will desert tonight? Who will surprise me with cowardice?

But later in the day, we receive heartening news. Finding the residents of Londinium in a state of chaotic apprehension at our approach, Paulinus abandoned the city rather than try to organize a defense. Those residents who could, followed him out.

"The city is virtually abandoned," my scouts tell me. "Paulinus's army is burdened by slow and panicked citizens. He is searching for a site to camp; he is not ready to face us."

The news travels quickly, and with it, jubilation. Londinium is ours for the taking. Londinium and its riches. But that is not what I am thinking. I should chase Paulinus, pursue him and surprise him on the road from behind. But, I argue with myself, he would have scouts; he would discover that we were coming, and he'd turn the army, unwieldy as it might be, around to face us. No. I've already made one mistake in choosing a road as a battlefield. I cannot make that mistake again. And my army, now, has momentum; I don't know if I could steer them away from Londinium. They want this prize, one more Roman town. And they will have it.

Leth agrees, but is tempted, as I am, to give chase. Carduc will not advise in terms of strategy but warns that I must have faith in my decision.

"Then it is Londinium," I say, as though I am confident. But in a moment, I am defending that decision as though it has been challenged. I am trying to convince myself. "We are on course to the city. I have promised Londinium. Paulinus has probably posted scouts along his route to detect us. Or worse, troops to ambush us." Leth nods; Carduc is silent. My arguments have only weakened my resolve. "Are there signs, Carduc?"

"When we set out for Camulodumnum, you asked me about signs. I told you then, the time for action is now. The Romans gave us all the signs we needed. Those are the signs I read, not the stars, not the course a hare takes when it darts from you, but the actions that people take, their decisions, the way one person answers another, looks at another."

"You read the sky for my father," I protest.

"No. You believed that of me. Your father did, too. I only read his face, his eyes, and the faces and eyes of those he dealt with."

"What would my father's face say now?"

"Your face says that you will take the army to Londinium."

And it says that I don't know if that is the right decision. I should chase Paulinus. I know it, but I am afraid of another costly mistake. And I don't know if I could persuade this army away from Londinium. My control of them is tenuous. I know that, too, and that is in my face. And Carduc reads it there, reads it all.

"We will take Londinium," I say, but I don't pretend to have conviction.

———

Londinium. We sweep through the city. The killing of those who stayed behind is merciless and gruesome. This army, in its anticipation of Paulinus over the last few days, has prepared itself to kill, and there are not enough Romans in Londinium to satisfy that preparedness. So, here limbs are hacked and littered around the village. The sacking is equally ruthless, and I make no attempt to curtail it. I promised them Londinium, and they take it with a vengeance.

———

"He will be looking for a battlesite," Leth observes of Paulinus as we wait out the looting.

"Yes," I agree, "and he'll choose one that gives him the advantage."

"He'll try to keep the site unknown to you until he has rested his army there for a day," Leth adds. "Then he'll send word, and we will have to travel to meet him. His army will be rested; ours will not."

"Then we must choose a site first," I decide. "And send him word that *we* are waiting. This is Catuvellauni territory. Find someone who knows the land here. Ask where there is a suitable site for a battle."

———

Later Leth returns with a description of a site a half-day's journey east of Londinium. Paulinus would have to turn his army around, and it would take him at least a day and a half to reach us there. He would arrive tired.

"A stream runs along the southern edge of the valley, and a forest flanks it. We could camp at the stream, take advantage of the running water," Leth elaborates.

"The stream is an advantage," I agree, and though I don't say it aloud, the forest is one, too. If Paulinus forces us into retreat, we can abandon wagons, and take to the woods. At least some of us will escape. This vision of us running reminds me of Coel, Leanan's husband, and I wonder if it's possible that he's emerged from the forest and is fighting with us, unknown to Leanan, unrecognized by those he camps with now. Perhaps he is near enough to watch her, to long to touch her. I remember so clearly that first flash of blue as I rode in the woods looking for Tallas–a streak, then gone. That was the start of everything. An instant of blue, and after it, nothing was the same.

I ask Leth to have the Catuvellauni party lead us.

I must pledge to my army that we will return to Londinium after we face Paulinus and collect whatever goods have not yet been claimed. I discover that at least three Iceni men are dead–killed by other Iceni–in an argument over a supply of wine. Though it is recklessly wasteful, I leave behind over a hundred men to guard the city, guard it against my own people. Without this precaution, some would stay behind collecting what was left. "Any looters," I command, "are to be killed and staked, just as the Roman women are staked. Let them be hanging here for all to see their shame when we return." Impaled Iceni bodies will greet us on our return, I am sure. This newly learned love of plunder is clearly already too great in some to surrender easily. And when this battle is over, and it is time to return home, some will still be unsatisfied and will ride from territory to territory seeking abandoned Roman towns and goods. And when there is nothing Roman left to take, where will they turn their avarice?

The Catuvellauni lead, and as estimated, we approach the site before nightfall. What will be the battlefield is clear enough, expansive, somewhat rocky, but generally flat.

"The valley?" I ask Aldric, the leader of the Catuvellauni tribesmen. "And the stream?"

With guards ringing us, Aldric, Carduc and I ride ahead over this ground that in a day or two will be blood-muddy.

"There," Aldric announces when we are holding the reins of our horses, looking downhill into the valley. He smiles with satisfaction, as though he himself placed the valley and stream in their positions. It is as he described with a stream running on the southern edge of the valley and a forest extending on three sides.

Leth observes that if we wait in the valley until Paulinus's arrival, we can keep the size of our army a mystery, though by now, Paulinus has undoubtedly been informed that our numbers are great. Still, keeping the army hidden is a good tactic, if only because it will cause Paulinus some confusion when he first arrives.

"You chose well," I tell Aldric. "We will face Paulinus here."

I urge the warriors to camp with their families–as this may be the last night for some of them–but many prefer the camaraderie of their fellow warriors on this eve before battle, our first true battle.

It is night when the camps are finally settled, and the wagons that were upset on their journeys down the hill have been righted, their contents collected.

I send messengers to suggest sacrifices. At our camp, Carduc unharnesses one of the oxen and leads it, lumbering, toward our fire. It is a generous offering and though would be better accepted if made by a Druid, it should satisfy the gods and bring us favor. I pray for strength, for ferocity. I promise a lifetime of honor and service for a victory. Tallas. He comes to mind when I should be thinking only of the gods. Apollo-Belinus. Forgive my weakness. I think of a man when I should be speaking to gods. Taranis. Icena. Be with me. Esus, accept this sacrifice. Andraste, guide me. Tallas, be with me. Are you with me?

When we have prayed and circled the ox three times, Carduc instructs me on the thrust of my sword. Just below its eyes, I force my blade, and with an exhalation of hot breath, the animal buckles to the ground. Carduc pushes it onto its side, then slits its length with his sword. Blood, stench, entrails leak. Carduc drops his sword and cups his hands near the throat catching a palmful of blood. He extends his careful hands toward my mouth, and tips them. I sip, hold the warm, thick fluid in my mouth; my throat will not accept it. My stomach is already retching, wanting to dispel it before it has even been delivered. I swallow. I am supposed to be strengthened by this draught, instead the blood makes me hot and sick. Unsteady. Katha is ready with water, water that in my mouth tastes of blood.

Later, after I have sent messengers to tell Paulinus that we await him, when I am lying on the ground with Neidriu and Grawnei, and the ox's blood has finally joined my own and stopped sickening me, Neidriu asks, "Why did you drink it?"

"To take the ox's strength."

"Did you? Take the strength?" She is hopeful.

"Yes."

"Will the fighting be over soon?"

"Yes."

Tentatively, she asks, "Is it because of us?"

"Because of you?"

"The fighting. Is it because of us?" She looks quickly to Grawnei, and then they both drop their eyes away from mine.

What should they be told? Yes? And let them carry the burden? No, when what has happened in the last weeks has had everything to do with what was done to them? "Rome has been mistreating us for a long time. The tribute, the killing of the priests, then what was done to you. They threatened to take all our land and make us slaves. You do have something to do with this. We all do. Every tribesmember has something to do with it. We have decided to fight. You helped us know that we should."

She is quiet again, then asks doubtfully, "Do you remember Father?"

"Of course I remember him. Why do you ask?"

"You rarely speak of him."

No. I do like to speak of him. I do not want to think of him, though he forces me to when his face comes to me when it is Tallas's face I want. Prasutagus, I did love you, and you knew I didn't want to.

"I remember his laugh, do you?" I ask. "It was a hearty laugh."

Neidriu sits up, excited at this skimpy homage to her father, knowing, in her sensitive way, that on this night of questionable futures, she needs to know about the past.

"Lie back down," I instruct. "He was tall and strong."

"Before he was sick," she remembers sadly.

"Before he was sick. Remember his moustache?"

"Down to here." Neidriu taps her chest.

"Yes."

"And his eyes?"

"Brown, like mine."

We remember–hair, smile, kindness, constancy. He still lives vividly in our memories. But his face will be forgotten, too, years from now. Maybe even sooner because memory is servant to death, and does the work of preparing us to see how spirit will be separated from body, how spirit–that which we really know of a person–endures while the body cannot. Grawnei listens as hungrily as Neidriu, perhaps already aware of the inexorable approach of forgetfulness. We remember the way he lifted them onto his horse, the way he gave them small duties. And thinking of them so young, I tell them about themselves as babies, and they are as happy to hear these stories. "You both always had things on your minds," I tell them. "I never knew what they were." I tell Neidriu of her nervousness, her discomfort in this world. I recall Grawnei's brooding.

"And then you grew out of your restlessness," I tell Neidriu. "You realized you had a sister, and you started following her around, wanting to do everything she did."

Neidriu giggles.

"If Grawnei spilled her milk, you'd spill a little. If she was sick, you had to be in bed too."

"Remember." Carduc has made me hate the word. But there is other remembering, better remembering. There was our happiness. We were happy. That is the truth. I was happy. I remember being happy. Under Rome's thumb and happy. In a marriage forced on me, yet happy. If only Catus Decianus hadn't come, couldn't we still be happy, even without Prasutagus? Catus Decianus. I remember. His back. Neidriu's foot.

"Mother," Neidriu sleepily calls me back. "Tell me more."

I shouldn't have been happy under Rome, shouldn't have believed in that happiness, shouldn't have not known that one day Rome would show its true self, that Decianus would come.

"No more, Neidriu. No more remembering for now. After, we will remember. After, when Rome is gone, we will remember. But for now I can tell another story, a story of sisters. Would you like that–a story about sisters?"

"Mm." She will be asleep soon.

"And you Grawnei, would you like that? You're so quiet, I could almost forget that you're here. But you don't want that, do you? You don't want me to forget you. No. And I could never forget you. Could I? No. Never."

"Two sisters," Neidriu interrupts, "like Grawnei and me."

"Yes, like Grawnei and you. But this was a time long ago. Before Rome." My daughters do not know a time before Rome. I do not know a time before Rome. But there was a time. Long ago. A time in stories. A time so long ago, it can only be remembered by stories.

"A baby girl was born to a woman, and a year later, another baby girl," I begin, remembering, remembering Katha telling me this story, remembering wanting a sister. "And though they were close in age, they were very different in appearance. One was fair, the other dark.

Day and Night, the mother called them, and that is what everyone else began to call them, too. The girls did not like these names. 'If I am Day,' said the youngest, 'and you are Night, then we cannot be together. Day must leave when Night comes, and Night must leave when Day arrives. It would be better if we were called Dawn and Dusk because at Dawn and Dusk, Night and Day hold hands in the sky and linger with one another.' But the oldest sister told the youngest not to worry. 'We are not really Day and Night. They are just names people call us. Look, we're together now,' she pointed out to her younger sister, 'and it is day, and tonight we will be together in our bed when it is night.'

"The younger girl was comforted. But now it happened that a farmer heard of the girls, and he got the idea that if there was no Night, and only Day, his crops would grow much quicker and fuller. He would have more to sell and could become a rich man. So, what do you think he did?"

I can see by Grawnei's expectant face that she can guess what happens next, but she will not say. I think that even if this were a different time, a time when Grawnei was speaking, she would not say; she loves her sister enough to let the story unfold for her.

"Grawnei knows," I say.

Neidriu looks at her but doesn't ask her to reveal what she knows. Her compassion for her sister prevents her from trying to coax or trick her into speaking. They have made some tacit agreement, and they trust each other in it, and it will probably be Neidriu that Grawnei first speaks to, if she ever does speak again.

"What happens?" Neidriu asks me. "Is it bad?"

"One day when the two sisters were out playing in the hills, the farmer came up behind them and dragged Night away with him. The girl called Day followed, but when she came to the farmer's fields, she did not see her sister. Day searched and searched, and then went home to get her mother. Together they returned to the farmer's land and pleaded for the return of Night, but the farmer denied taking her and forced them off his land. The mother was so upset at the loss of her dark-haired daughter that she became ill. But Day would not give up.

While her mother went home, Day hid in the farmer's fields hoping that she would find some hint as to where her sister might be. Late in the afternoon, she heard the farmer speaking to his crop of wheat. 'Now you will grow tall,' he sang happily. 'Without Night to slow your growth, you will be abundant soon and ready for harvest. When I sell you, you will bring me great profits. I will be the richest man in the land.'

"When Day heard this, she understood why the man had hidden her sister away. She came out of her hiding place and called to the farmer, 'Sir,' she said politely, 'you have made a mistake. My sister is not really the night. She is just called that because of her dark eyes and hair. Hiding her away will have no effect on your crops. Night will come. Look at the sky. You can see the sun setting.' But the farmer pretended not to know what the girl was talking about, and chased her away from his fields.

"Now the sister had an idea. She realized that if the farmer's crop did not grow well then he would understand that it was of no use to keep Night locked up. So even though the girl did not like the idea of destroying the farmer's crop–she didn't want to see him starve– she had no choice. She ran home, lit a torch in the hearth fire and returned to the farmer's fields. Because it hadn't rained in several days, much of the farmer's wheat was dry, and caught fire easily. The farmer smelled the fire and came running out to his fields, but he couldn't stop the flames from spreading. By morning, at least half of his crop was ruined.

"While the farmer was surveying the damage and shaking his head in dismay, Day approached him. 'Farmer,' she said. 'Before you send me away, listen to what I have to tell you. You have hidden Night in the hope that Day would yield you a better crop. But you see that without Night, Day shines too brightly and dries and burns your crop. Unless you want to lose the rest of the field, then you must free Night. Return her to me, and I, Day, will stop burning your wheat.'

"The farmer submitted to Day, and released Night from the pit he had dug for her. The sisters hugged and cried; they were so happy to see one another. And when they returned home, their mother was so glad to see her daughters together that she jumped out of bed and was well again."

Neidriu moans sleepily, "What happened to the farmer?"

"The farmer had a small harvest, but enough to live on, and he never bothered the sisters again."

"I like that," Neidriu affirms.

"Now sleep." I kiss them each. But I am not ready to join them, and when they sleep, I get up and assist Katha with the preparations of the ox meat. She is planning stews for the tough flesh.

"I'll tear some of this up for the pups," she says.

I don't answer, and she is quiet, and I work by her until a rare calm settles on me. When the task is complete, we bid each other good night with a hug and say nothing of the things that are in our hearts, nothing of things we might say though we know tomorrow could be our last day together.

When I lie down again, my calm abandons me, and images of the imminent battle keep me from sleeping. I see myself with my sword. I see Romans. Blood. Their blood? I pray again to Andraste but, again, prayers make me want to call on Tallas.

Remember.

But like his face, memories have begun to abandon me. He and I are by the river so many years ago. But there were other times besides that time. Why can't I recall them now? He and I are by the river. His weight is on me.

I put my wrist to my mouth, try to remember his neck against my lips.

In the morning, messengers bring me news of Garan. He has named himself king and laid claim to Iceni territory, letting it be known that he will relinquish the land to Paulinus but not to me. So, Paulinus is not to be my final foe. And whom, after Garan?

Paulinus keeps us waiting. Afternoon into evening. Will he come during the night? I sit by the fire, but do not light it. "No fires tonight." I've sent out word. If he comes, let him come to darkness. If he plans a night attack, we will not light the way for him.

Guards watch the hill. We are ready.

And he makes us wait.

Katha and Carduc. Leth. Leanan. We wait. Our thoughts private, unspoken.

The sky is low and murky. Not a star. Tomorrow it will rain. Tomorrow. We will live tomorrow, or we will die. Rain, yes, my wounds ache. What wounds will I earn tomorrow? What sewing will Katha do? And tomorrow night, when it is over, who will gather here around the fire that we light? Carduc? With a wound? Leth?

What is that sound we strain toward?

Hooves? "Carduc, is that hooves?"

"Thunder," he determines.

Thunder.

But I am up; I thought the sound was hooves, and my body pounds with the mistake. Hooves. No. Thunder. Just thunder. But now I must be ready. "Katha, I must ask you, has Carduc given you a pouch, a pouch with herbs for my daughters?"

She reaches under her cloak and shows me. A small sack. Ordinary. Tied at her waist.

"If I..." What are the words for this? "If I am killed, if Rome defeats us... if you see that happening, give them a drink with the herbs. But be sure, Katha. Be sure that it is hopeless. Wait long enough to be sure, but not so long that a Roman soldier can get to them. Do you understand? Promise me, Katha. Don't cry. Promise me that Rome will never handle my daughters again. Promise me."

"You ask a terrible thing of me," she cries.

"Promise me."

"I promise you."

"Now sit again and give me your hand. Close to me. Yes. This hand, and the other, too. Give them to me. And take mine. And hold hard, Katha."

At dawn, Paulinus comes.

TWENTY-FIVE

A steady rain.
    Ready.
    A shriek. Shrieks.
    To the hill.
    And up.
    And over the ridge.
    Chariots. Horses. Warriors, naked, blued.
    Flying toward them. Toward Rome.
    See us come.
    My sword lands on leather. Splits it, finds flesh. Pliant. And blood.
    They fight well.
    We fight well.
    We push them back.
    Leather and flesh give.
    Blood.
    How long? Already my arms tire.
    We push them back.
    Is this their strength? All of their strength?
    Then victory is possible. It is possible.
    Is it possible?
    Rain.
    And rain.

Where is Paulinus? The man. A single man.

The ground puckers, sucks at the hooves. Movement is slowed. Mud and blood. Bodies.

Now they cease to fall back. Do they? I can't tell. No. They don't fall back.

A steady thump–hooves on the soft cloying earth, or my own blood, hard in my ears?

Two hands to steady the sword. There, I catch a Roman horse across its snout. Its head bounces furiously. I swing again, and get the Roman this time where neck meets shoulder. He never falls from the horse.

Carduc? Leth?

A trumpet blares. Now they retreat. Seem to retreat, fall back.

What? Do they fall back?

The rain continues. Less heavily now.

Bodies.

Another Roman chest opens against my sword.

But then they are a wall. The Roman wall. Fresh soldiers. From where? Alert. Quick. Shields overlapping. Impenetrable. Impenetrable Rome.

Now we are pushed.

Yes?

Back.

Yes.

And close. Why are we cramming together? Why aren't we fanning out? "Spread out." We should be surrounding them, making them face us on many fronts. Individually. The way we fight best. "Spread out. Surround them."

But they push us.

Too many bodies. The ground is flesh and snapping bones.

My horse hooves a fallen tribesman, and another. Its ankles twist on the ghastly terrain.

Forgive us for the abuse of these bodies of our warriors.

I hear it before I feel it–a thin whistle. I am still hearing it when it sears into my shoulder, unbalances me. Sharp shudder of pain.

I fall. Land against a body. Tribesman. Hooves, nearby. I curl to protect myself. The arrow snaps. Sticky blood of this man's naked hip against my cheek.

A foot on me.

And another.

I curl away.

Then, I am pulled. Standing. Led, running, pushing aside my own people. Pushing them roughly. Get out of the way. Make way. A tribesman has me by the arm. The other arm, I cradle. Blood. Another tribesman pulls me to his horse, and rides me away. Until there is air again. Until I can breathe. Along the battlefield toward the ridge.

Then I see it.

My view can only take in the east side, but when I see what is happening there, I know with dreadful certainty that it is happening on the west, too. Rome is spreading their line, spreading it and bending it, bending it in on the east side and surely in on the west side, intending to, in fact beginning to squeeze us into its center, constructing a bucket of soldiers around us, forcing us into the bucket, making us face them on three sides, closing us in, limiting our space, making our long swords unwieldy.

They will push us to the ridge and over. They will push us to the ridge and over.

I see the plan, so well executed and then... blue flash. A memory calling itself to life. But it is not a memory. It is blue flesh, blue and bloodied. It is terror and despair. An Iceni warrior darting for the ridge, perhaps struck by the same realization of Rome's strategy that has just struck me. Perhaps just afraid–no realization–just fear, persistent, loud, then louder fear.

Stop. But he is at the ridge.

Stop. And over the ridge. To a wagon. He will find his family, have his wounds tended.

But no. He seeks no one, has an opening in sight, leaps through into the woods. Gone.

Gone.

And now I see something else, something that, for a moment, deadens the air around me. Our wagons, our families in the valley, at the edge of the forest, lining the edge of the forest, block the way into the forest. Block our escape. If we need escape. The wagons. Our families. Our own wagons. Our own families are in our path of escape.

The tribesman rides me over the ridge. Toward our wagon. Our wagon in the way of escape.

"Katha."

She rushes toward me. Katha.

The tribesman spills me off the horse, into her arms; she leads me to the wagon.

"Cut the skin and remove the arrowhead," I demand.

First, with a cloth, she clears my face.

"Sit," she tells me.

"Just do it," I insist. My eyes on the ridge. "Do it." We must retreat. Pull ourselves out of the bucket Rome has confined us in. Move to the ridge. Hold the ridge. Hold them back.

She seems to take her time, heating the knife, dabbing the wound. "Look away," she warns.

When she digs into my flesh, it is a pain equal to that which the fast arrow made. I will not cry out. I will not. Katha. Katha. "Katha." My hand goes up to protect my wound.

"There," she says. She cleans it again, and begins sewing.

I vomit between my legs. Always vomit at pain. Weak stomach. Weak Boudicca.

When she is done, I rest. "Just for a moment. A moment." My body insists, trembles for rest; my eyes close.

How long? How long did I sleep? I shouldn't have slept. I stand, too quickly, and a blackness pours over my eyes. Then clears, and I steady myself. I see now that many of the camps are busy with wounded. And there are more on the hill. More coming over the ridge.

"You need more rest," Katha says firmly. Can she tell how badly the battle goes?

"I cannot," I answer gently, and she does not insist.

Retreat. We must retreat. Pull ourselves away. Then hold the ridge.

Painfully, I mount a fresh horse, feel the wound pull and know my arms are too weak to use my sword effectively. Still, I must go.

"Mother."

I see her fear. So much fear.

"Stay in the wagon, Neidriu," I shout, though my voice is weak, and I don't know if it carries to her. "You, too, Grawnei." I look to Katha. Should she take them and run? Into the woods? "Where is Leanan?" I ask. She should join them.

Katha nods toward the battlefield. "She wanted to fight."

"I saw Carduc," I assure her. "He's alive."

"I know." She puts her hand to her chest and taps it to tell me she has a feeling there, a knowledge.

"Katha..."

A thundering at the ridge draws our eyes upward. Now the hill is thick with wounded, with running. Rome is at the ridge. "Rome is at the ridge."

So quickly.

"Rome." A warning goes up. "Rome."

There is sudden and chaotic movement in the camps; wagons are pulled, turned, abandoned as families realize they block their own escape. They need escape.

"Mother," Neidriu cries again. "Mother," she pleads. "Mama."

From her face to the hill, from the hill to her face, I look, decide. "Apollo-Belinus, curse them. Minerva, curse them. Curse them. Let their empire burn. Leave us alone. Leave us alone. Why couldn't they leave us alone?"

"Boudicca..."

"Katha," now I whisper, "the herbs."

Curse Rome. Curse their empire. Curse their dead. Always coming. Always pushing us.

She has the small sack ready at her waist. "Wormwood and hops," she says hoarsely, handing me the pouch.

"Is there milk?"

"No. Mead."

"Get me two cups." I go to the wagon, hold my daughters' hands as they jump down. "Come and have a drink with me. Then I have to go back to the battle. Here. Sit here." Facing the woods, away from the hill. Away from Rome. Still, we can see the running. Blue flesh. Bloody flesh. Muddied.

"Why do they run?" Neidriu asks, though the thinness of her voice and the brightness of her eyes tell me that she knows why.

"Shh." I try to speak calmly. "Hush, little one. Do you know that Katha called me 'little one'?"

Neidriu nods. "You told me."

"Good. And what did we decide on as a name for your sister? Grawnei, what was it? Come closer. Right next to me. That's better. As if we're in bed together. Side by side."

Katha brings the mead; a terrible sorrow dims her face.

"Smile at Katha. Tell her you love her."

Neidriu obliges, and her sweet obedience fills my chest with a sob.

"Now," I take a breath, suppress the wail. "Now, we will have a drink together. I want your company." With a reluctant hand, I shake some of the powder into each cup. "This is a special mix of herbs, just for you. It will make you sleep, and when you awaken, the battle will be over."

Over.

"I don't like mead," Neidriu whimpers.

"You'll drink it for me, little one. So will Grawnei. There will be milk later. Lots of milk. Now be brave. It's only bitter. First, here, kiss me, let me kiss you. I love you. You know that, don't you? This is best for you. You don't have to be afraid. Nothing will hurt you. You will just sleep." I kiss Neidriu on her warm head, on each eye, on her dry lips, on her neck. My hungry affection frightens her.

"Mama?" She is a baby again.

"Now, Grawnei. Come, you are not too big for your mother's kisses." I kiss her the same way. "When you awaken, you will speak. Your fears, your shame will be forgotten."

She looks at me with some alarm. With understanding? Does she know what I am about to do? "Can you say a word?" I beg, as if a word

197

from her could change everything. Then, "Never mind. It's all right. It is all right. Rome will not hurt you again." Her eyes, are they pleading? No, I will not do it. Grawnei, I cannot do it.

But I must. I must force myself. I am her mother. Their mother. And I must protect her. "Remember." Was it two men who left her room that day? I must think of her in Roman hands. Roman hands on her, abusing her. No. I must, Grawnei. I must. I will protect you this time. "Drink now. It's all right."

"Will you drink, Mama?" Neidriu asks.

Grawnei waits for the answer.

"I have to return to battle, but I will have a cup of mead. Katha."

She brings another cup. "There is enough for you," I tell her, "and Carduc. Leanan too."

Katha understands. "Leanan still hopes to find her sons."

"And you?"

"I will wait."

For Carduc. But he will be dead. We will all be dead.

"Sip it, Neidriu. There, it isn't so bad. And you, Grawnei, sip, too. And another sip. That's how we'll do it. A sip and a sip. Go again. Neidriu, your turn. Grawnei. Until it is finished. Two girls, two sisters. Do you remember the story I told you the other night? Would you like to hear another? Yes, about sisters. Two sisters..." I keep talking, wanting them to hear my voice when they begin to drift away. The hops will make them sleepy, hopefully, before the poison chokes their lives. How quick is it? How much time do I have with them?

"My pup," Neidriu says. I can see that she is already sickened by the drink. Come, sleep, before the poison convulses her. "I don't like the mead."

"Drink a little more. Come on. I'll have Katha bring the pups. Come on. Would you like that? Another sip. Good girl. Grawnei. Good."

Neidriu gags. Do not vomit. "All right, that's enough for now. Katha," I call, "bring the pups. Hurry." I look away from my daughters for a moment to the hill. Rome is visible. Always visible. Soon they will be upon us. I should return. Those who are still fighting should see me die in battle. Yes.

But no. No. I cannot leave my daughters. I will not die on the end of a short sword. Rome will not kill me. You will not kill me. I will not let you. I will die with my daughters. Gods, forgive me my cowardice.

When Katha has brought the pups and Neidriu and Grawnei are each holding one close, I turn the small sack over my mead and use a finger to mix it. "There is still enough left." I hand the pouch to Katha who is watching me with such sadness. We are dying. We are still breathing and still looking at one another but our lives have ended. All of us, dying. "Iceni." Just a word. A people, once.

"I will wait," Katha says again.

"Don't wait long," I warn. "They will be merciless." We were a people once. Iceni. And now, we will be dead. All of us dead or slaves. And it is my doing. My vengeance. My pride. We could have given them the land; we could have worked it. We were complacent once; I was complacent once. We could have been complacent again. Forget. That is what I should have done. Forget. Not remember. Forget about the rapes. Forget about the rapes. We would have been left alive. But remember. "Remember." "Remember" became my language. "Remember" let me kill my people. "Remember" is forcing me to kill my daughters. "Remember." But we will be forgotten.

Grawnei takes another sip, then lets her pup lap from her cup. Neidriu does what her sister does.

"You first," I scold. "I'll drink, too. Then we'll all sleep. But first a prayer. Bless us. Protect us. Forgive us." I take a small sip, wanting to be sure before I drink more that Neidriu and Grawnei are safe. Their only safety now is in their deaths. There is commotion all around, and I draw them closer, shielding them from it, distracting them. Neidriu complains that she does not feel well. Good, I think. "Now, sleep." I hold her cup and force one more sip. She swallows, then grimaces. "Here, put your head on my lap." She curls into me.

"A story," she murmurs.

"A story? Yes, but first your sister must take another sip. Grawnei, one more sip." She drinks, finishing what is in her cup. "Good." A story. What story is there to tell now? "Let me take another sip." I gulp my mead, then pat my thigh, and Grawnei lies down there. "Now, hold my hand. Let me take your hands, and I will think of a story. Little one? Neidriu?" She doesn't make any sound. "Grawnei? What will you dream of, Grawnei?" I ask, letting my tears fall. "Let's tell a story of your dream. Of a place you can go where you will see your father. Are you cold? Here, come closer. Grawnei? Grawnei? Can you forgive me? I could not protect you. Can you forgive me? Neidriu? Grawnei?" My daughters. My daughters. "Katha. Katha."

She comes. It must be her. I feel her arms around my neck. I smell her, but I cannot see her. I am holding their hands to my face, over my eyes. Do not let me see what I have done. Do not let me see this world again. Where is my poison?

But no, it must wait. It must wait. "Katha."

"Yes. Yes. I'm here."

"Quickly, Katha we must get them back to the wagon. Quickly. And then burn it. Do you hear me? Burn it. Don't let the Romans at them. Don't let them lie here. Katha..."

Now there is a last rage in me. Paulinus. "Paulinus." When their bodies are in the wagon, my daughters' bodies, I mount a horse.

Paulinus. I will find Paulinus. I will kill him. Kill Rome. He will die for my daughters' deaths. He will die.

The ground is hard when I hit it, then wet. And cool. And I have stopped falling. This sleep will be good. I can feel its depth. Its dark depth. The ground is fine against my cheek.

Tallas. I saw you fall. Or did I only dream it? Your cheek against the ground. But where is your face? And your eyes? Were they green? Or blue when you fell? Green or blue when they killed you? Why don't I know? Green. Did I see them? And Grawnei's. Grawnei's. Did I see hers? Were they green when she closed them? I must see them. And Neidriu's. Brown. I know they are brown, but let me see them once more. And their faces, once more. Once more. So I don't forget. Never forget.

I'm coming. I'm coming, Grawnei. Neidriu. Wait for me. I'll come. And I'll tell you a story. Do you want a story? I will tell you a story.

ABOUT THE AUTHOR

While studying Celtic culture, Joann Smith became fascinated by Boudicca. The Celts did not keep written records, so all accounts of Boudicca's rebellion come from Roman sources. Joann wanted to give Boudicca a voice, and so she wrote this novel.

Joann has published many short stories in various literary journals, including: *servinghouse journal; Chagrin River Review; New York Stories; The Greensboro Review; The Best of Writers at Work; Literal Latte; Image: A Journal of Art and Religion;* and others. Her story published in *Image* was selected as one of the 100 Notable Stories by the editors of *Best American Short Stories 2000.* She earned an M.F.A in Fine Arts from Sarah Lawrence College and an M.A. in English from Lehman College, CUNY.

When I Was Boudicca is her first novel.

To learn more the author, visit her website: www.write-goals.com

Printed in Great Britain
by Amazon

12517701R00119